FIND
A
STRANGER,
SAY
GOODBYE

FIND A STRANGER, SAY GOODBYE

LOIS LOWRY

Houghton Mifflin Company Boston 1978

For Kristin

1

"IF YOU GET a fat letter, it means you've been accepted. If you get a thin letter, forget it."

Becky Margeson made the pronouncement. No one was really listening; they'd all heard it before. It was part of the college-admissions folklore that circulated every spring. It was one of the myths that had been disproved two years before when the president of the student council had been accepted by an Ivy League college and didn't know it for a week — didn't know it until his mother emptied the trash and found the (thin) crumpled letter, unopened, where he had thrown it in anger.

Natalie Armstrong, especially, wasn't listening to the two friends who were sprawled in her bedroom on the spring Saturday. Natalie had been thinking about something else for a long time, something that she hadn't told even her closest friends.

"Even if I get a letter six inches thick," groaned Gretchen Zimmerman, "it has to say 'scholarship' at the end of it, or I can't go." She nudged her sneakers off with alternate toes and examined her feet in the sunlight that came through Natalie's windows. "I wish it were summer, so I could get a tan. My feet look like haddock filets."

"I hate this waiting." Becky sighed. "Wait for the middle of April, to see if you've been accepted. Wait for summer, to get a tan. Then wait for summer to end, so you can go to college. Then what? I suppose you get there and end up waiting for the next thing."

"To get married." Gretchen grinned. She folded her bare feet under her and scrutinized her hands, spreading the fingers to imagine a wedding ring on one.

"Ha," snorted Natalie, with disdain.

"Ha," mimicked Gretchen, laughing. "You'll probably marry Paul the minute he graduates from college, Nat. You're so lucky."

"Lucky?" Natalie looked at her in surprise.

"You are, Nat," said Becky seriously. "Look at you. You're so gorgeous. Honestly, if I didn't like you so much I'd hate you. Has your face ever broken out, I mean *ever*?

Natalie laughed. "I had a cold sore once. My dad said it was caused by a virus."

"A cold sore. Big deal. I'm talking about zits. I've never known anyone who doesn't have zits except you." Becky leaned toward the mirror over Natalie's bureau, glanced at her own face, stuck out her tongue, and sighed.

"And you have Paul," mused Gretchen. "And you've already been accepted at MacKenzie. And your parents can afford the tuition. God, you *are* lucky, Nat. Did your application form have one of those stupid questions on it: 'What do you consider the most interesting thing about yourself?' What did you put, Nat: 'The most interesting thing about me is that I'm incredibly lucky'?"

Natalie crumpled up a piece of notebook paper and threw it halfheartedly at Becky. "No," she said. "I put, 'The most interesting thing about me is that my best friends are insane'!"

They all laughed.

It was the kind of day when it was easy to laugh at

things. The snow had melted at last, and the early April sun was the sort that promised summer before long. The hardest parts of senior-year classes were over; they were all marking time, and the teachers indulged them. The English teacher had assigned Hawthorne and Thoreau in the fall, and now they were reading Salinger and Vonnegut. Four years of French conjugations had been laid, pretty much, to rest, and the French teacher was teaching them something about cuisine. Some days they borrowed the Home Ec room and made crêpes. Sometimes they read the magazine *Elle* in class, and talked about fashion; the boys groaned and made vomiting gestures in the aisles between the desks, when they weren't flipping the pages and looking for see-through blouses.

Becky and Gretchen would both get into college, and Gretchen, who had the highest College Board scores in the history of the high school, would win the scholarships that would make it possible for her to go.

Paul had been accepted, already, at Yale. That was a long distance from MacKenzie, but it didn't seem important. She would see him during vacations; they would write; they would stay close; and they both looked forward to new things.

The springtime agonizing was just part of the senior ritual, part of the boredom. Something to talk about while they waited for time to pass.

There was a knock on Natalie's bedroom door. Nancy, her sister, stuck her head inside. Nancy was a year younger: sixteen, chubby, blond, and freckled. The yearbook would, next year, describe Nancy as "cute as a button." It had already described Natalie with the quotation "She walks in beauty." They were not at all alike. But they were friends.

"Mom wants you to set the table, Nat."

"Nancy, do me a favor?"

"Mmmmm?"

"Bug off."

Nancy grinned and closed the door.

"Well, listen," said Gretchen, standing up. "I have to go anyway."

"Me too," said Becky. "Gotta go check the mail at home."

"Tell Mom I'll be down in a minute," Natalie said, and listened to the muted thuds of her friends' feet on the carpeted stairs, to Nancy's called "See ya!" and to the front door's open and close.

She sat where she was, and noticed that she could see herself in the wall mirror across the room. Her long dark hair. The startlingly blue eyes. Her skin was very light now, but she would tan easily and early in the summer. Her teeth were even and straight; she had never needed the braces that Nancy had worn, now, for three years.

They're right, I guess. I *am* lucky. That is, if looks are what count. I suppose I'm good-looking. And I'm bright enough that I don't have to study much, that I got into college, that I'll probably get into med school.

I can do whatever I want.

Then why do I want something that scares me so much?

Natalie walked over to her desk, the pine desk that her father had built for her in his garage workshop, years before. It was marred now, and scratched, but she loved it still, as she had the day he finished the final sanding and rubbed in the wax carefully with a soft cloth.

Her father, a doctor, was very dear to her. In kindergarten and the early grades of elementary school, when she had made him paperweights and penwipers every Father's Day (and who uses paperweights or penwipers? Nobody, she knew now, as she hadn't, then) he had given them places of honor on his desk as if they were truly objets d'art. It was he who had bandaged the scraped knees of her childhood, bathed her in cool, medicated baths when she itched all over from chicken pox, and had been the one beside her bed, holding her hand, when she woke after a long night of pain and drugged sleep to find her appendix gone.

Kay Armstrong, Natalie's mother, was the volatile one in the family. The daughter of gypsylike, artistic parents, Kay had traveled as a child in Europe and Mexico; had absorbed her parents' passion for color, light, and change; and had inherited their exuberant emotions. She had settled as a young woman for the quiet, uncomplicated life of a small-town doctor's wife because she loved Alden Armstrong; but she brought to the family spontaneity and vibrancy that startled them all, at times. The Armstrong household was not like any other, and it was because of Kay.

It was the only house in Branford, Maine, for example, that had, in the modern, copiously tiled upstairs bathroom, an immense old-fashioned bathtub, with feet, in the center of the room. And the feet had Crimson Passion polish on each toe. Kay Armstrong had painted it there, meticulously, herself one October afternoon when all the other doctors' wives in Branford were listening to a speaker discuss The Art of Flower Arranging after their monthly luncheon, to which she had forgotten to go.

She was the only doctor's wife in Branford, Maine, who hung her wash on an outdoor clothesline instead of putting it through a dryer, because she liked to look out the window and see the clothes blowing in the wind. She had been especially delighted, one day, when one sleeve of the top of her husband's pajamas, prodded by the stiff breeze off the bay, reached over and grabbed her nightgown around the waist.

"I bet that's the sexiest thing that's ever happened in this back yard," she had exclaimed, watching in glee from the kitchen window.

"*Mother!*" groaned Nancy. "Don't be gross!"

"Well." Her mother grinned. "If you know of anything more than *that* that's been going on back there, I hope you've consulted your father about birth control."

"*Mother!*" groaned Nancy again. Kay Armstrong had grinned and shrugged, still watching the striped sleeve making sporadic breeze-guided passes at the pink nightgown.

She was not your run-of-the-mill mother. Natalie adored her.

Natalie called downstairs from the door of her bedroom. "Mom! I'll be down in a few minutes to set the table, okay?"

"Yo," called her mother affably.

Yo. Natalie smiled. That's Marine talk, she thought.

Who else . . . who else in the world has a mother who talks like a boot camp Marine?

She went to the desk, opened the top drawer, took out the paper that was there, looked at it briefly, and sighed.

Yo. Her mother had not said "Yo" when she read that paper. Her mother's face had crumpled like an old Kleenex, and her mother had cried.

And her father had turned away, his face set in the stiff and puzzled lines that formed there when he had a patient he could not help. "Natalie," he had said, and the word, her name, was almost a question. It was filled with pain.

They had not spoken of it again. Natalie had always felt that there was nothing she could not discuss with her parents. They had talked, often, over the years, about feelings: about anger, about grief, about love. But they had read the paper, when she gave it to them, and she had seen all those same feelings in their faces; she had seen their anguish, as well. And it was something they had not been able to talk about.

It had been two months. They had not mentioned it. Life went on in the Armstrong home, in combinations made up of Nancy's boisterous cheer, Natalie's more introspective calm, Kay Armstrong's splashes of color and craziness, and the doctor's dignity that kept them all moving in smooth and well-directed currents. But there was an undercurrent to the life, now. The murky hurt she had inflicted hung like a translucent curtain; they all looked through it, around it, over and under it, and pretended that it had never been hung there at all.

Once her father's sister, Horrible Aunt Helen, had sent them a hideous ceramic lamp for Christmas. It was a pale green panther with a dim bulb suspended from his under-side. If they placed it on top of the television, Horrible Aunt Helen had explained in her enclosed note, their eyes would be protected from damage that was likely to ensue from the flickering light of the screen.

"This guy is going to have terrible sexual problems," Natalie's mother had said, holding the panther upside down to examine the bulb and its dangling electric cord. "Why don't we just pack him up again and send him to Masters and Johnson in St. Louis?"

"Kay," her husband had said, "Helen stops here unan-nounced all the time. We have to put it on the TV, at least for a while, so we don't hurt her feelings."

"All right," said Mrs. Armstrong. She moved the small piece of Peruvian sculpture that had always stood on top of the television, and put the panther in its place. "But we shall consider it invisible."

They all looked at the panther. It was posed in a sinuous lunge, its fangs exposed. It was very large. Very, very green.

"Do you see a panther on top of the television?" asked Kay Armstrong.

"Nope." Nancy, who always caught the tail of her mother's fancies as they flew past, giggled. "Can't see a thing."

"A panther?" asked Natalie solemnly. "On the TV? Who in their right mind would have a panther on their TV?"

"Not the Armstrongs," said their father resolutely. "The Armstrongs are very tasteful people. I see nothing on the television at all."

The green panther had stayed there for a month. One afternoon Natalie, in her room, had heard a crash. When she went downstairs, her mother was picking up green ceramic pieces and dropping them into a wastebasket.

"Isn't it amazing," Kay Armstrong had said calmly, "how when something is invisible you are very apt to bump into it very hard with your elbow?"

"Amazing." Natalie grinned, helping her with the last green bits.

Now they were all playing the game again. If they pretended the paper didn't exist, it wouldn't exist.

But it does, Natalie thought. I had to write it. I had to ask them to read it.

And they will have to talk to me about it. Even if it hurts.

2   MACKENZIE COLLEGE'S APPLICATION blank had not been very different from any of the others. After the routine questions about Natalie's high school grades and activities, and after all the information about SATs, CEEBs, BOGs, and PCSs that sometimes made the whole college application procedure seem like something left glued to the bottom of the bowl when the alphabet soup was all gone, they had the question for which they had left an entire page of blank space.

Most colleges did. It was usually a question about the most interesting or meaningful thing that had happened to the applicant in the past few years. It was a question that panicked Branford, Maine, high school seniors and their guidance counselor, because nothing very exciting happened in Branford, Maine.

They all were very, very sure that the rest of the country was filled with high school seniors who had spent their summers working in leper colonies.

One summer, a pack of wild, rabid dogs had menaced the town of Branford before they were lured into a fenced area and shot by members of the state police. In truth, it was only four wild dogs traveling together; one of them, it was later found in the state laboratory, *did* have rabies. They had killed numerous chickens and one small calf in a pasture before they were destroyed. It had been a frightening two days; the townspeople were warned, by radio and TV and by police vehicles with loudspeakers, not to venture far from their houses. Small children were kept indoors until the danger was over. Branford high school boys had volunteered to help in tracking the dogs; in Maine, most teen-aged boys were experienced in tracking deer during hunting season. But the state police had refused the offer. Some of the boys had gone out on their own anyway, and one of them had shot the Episcopal minister's Saint Bernard by mistake. Of the five boys involved, none would tell which one had done it; they were all ordered home. They pooled their savings and bought Father Simms, who was reasonable about the whole thing, a new puppy, which he named Expiation and called Pete for short.

The incident nourished Mr. Flanagan, the high school guidance counselor, for two years. When seniors asked his advice on answering the big question of their applications, his eyes lit up. "Tell about the time the whole town stalked the rabid dog pack," he would say.

After a while, no one reminded him anymore that it had been three policemen shooting four dogs in a fenced yard. Most of the kids found themselves writing about the French Club's weekend trip to Quebec. Some preferred to tell of the time that the shack in which the local derelict lived, on the outskirts of town, burned to the ground with him in it; the Athletic Club had sponsored a quick raffle to raise money for his burial, and the entire high school turned out for the funeral. Most of the boys, at one time or another, had paid Willie, the derelict, a quarter to buy them a six-pack of beer. They didn't include that information on the college applications, but they liked to write about how the Branford Glee Club had spontaneously sung, "Where Have All the Flowers Gone" as what was left of Willie was laid to rest.

MacKenzie's application had worded the big question a little differently from most. Their question read, "What is the one thing about you that makes you different from the nine hundred high school seniors who will apply, this year, for admission to MacKenzie's freshman class? How will that one quality affect your life in the next four years?"

Natalie had looked at the question for a long time. Then she had taken a yellow legal pad from her desk, uncapped her fountain pen, and written,

The one thing that makes me different is that I have no idea who I really am.

My name is Natalie Chandler Armstrong. I was named for my mother's mother, Natalie Chandler, who is a famous sculptor. She was married to a painter who died before I was born, and they traveled all over the world. They were both very well known. My mother, who was their only child, is not a famous person, but she is artistic, like her parents, and tells fascinating stories about growing up with such an unusual family.

My father, Alden Armstrong, is a very dedicated doctor. He graduated from Harvard Medical School and worked for a while at the Lahey Clinic in Boston before he decided to come to Maine. For a while he was the only medical doctor in our small town. Today there are others, but one wing of our local hospital is named Armstrong after my father. Two years ago, people who had been my father's patients during his twenty years in Branford got together and raised the money to help pay for it and to name it in his honor. It makes me very proud to see his name there.

My younger sister, Nancy, looks exactly like my father, but she has my mother's personality. It's a nice combination.

But my parents adopted me when I was five days old. Of course I have developed characteristics that are like theirs, because they have been my family for seventeen years. But my real parentage is a complete mystery to me. Somewhere there are two people who created me, and I don't know who they are. I have dark brown hair, and light blue eyes. Genetically, that's an unusual combination. Where does it come from? I don't know.

Sometimes I lie awake at night, wondering what the story is behind my birth. Why would anyone give away a baby? Why did they give me away? It makes me angry, puzzled, and sad. Somewhere, I think, it must make them feel the same way. I can't believe that they have forgotten me.

I am sure that this will affect me not only for the next four years, but for my entire life, at least until I find the answers.

I intend to work very hard at college, because I want to be a doctor like my father. But at the same time, I have determined that I am going to try to find my natural parents. I don't know how. But I am sure there must be a way.

The essay, written in Natalie's small, meticulous handwriting, covered the entire sheet of extra-length paper. After she had written it, she set it aside.

On a second sheet, she began again.

The one thing that makes me different is that I want so much to be a good doctor. For two summers I have worked in my father's office, learning how to do simple lab tests, and watching how he deals with patients who entrust their lives and their health to him.

She went on, and filled the second sheet. It was the second essay that she copied carefully onto the application form, and mailed to MacKenzie College.

But it was the first one that she had shown her parents.

"*Why?*" her mother had asked, shaken. "Why, Natalie? What does it matter? You've been our daughter since you were an *infant*. Your father and I never think about the fact that you were adopted. Have we done something wrong? Have we made you feel different?"

Natalie had shook her head, biting her lip, mutely. There was no way to explain something she didn't really understand herself. But the feeling was there: the need. She looked at her father, hoping he could help them all. But his face was troubled, too.

"Nat," he had said, finally, "I don't know what to say. I think this search will be a terrible mistake on your part. What possible good could come of it?"

"I don't know," she told them softly. "I don't know. Except that the secrets would be gone."

The word made her father angry. *"Secrets?* Natalie, your mother and I have kept no secrets from you. We know nothing of your natural parents. That's how it should be. Your adoption was arranged through professionals who never disclosed that information to us. Nor did we ask them to. You became our daughter as much as Nancy did, a year later. And as far as we're concerned, there isn't any difference between the two of you. You were conceived; born; you entered our lives; became our daughters."

"It *isn't* the same. Nancy was conceived by you, born to you. Don't tell me that's the same. Who was *I* born to? Why did they give me away?

Her mother touched her hair. "Natalie. Those things don't matter. Really, they don't."

"They do," Natalie insisted. "They do to me."

"Nat," said her father finally, "let your mother and me talk about this together. Right now we're both upset. Give us time, and then we'll all discuss it again."

Natalie nodded reluctantly, and the translucent curtain came down between them. In the two months since their conversation, her parents had not mentioned it again.

3

IT WAS MAY, and she was arguing with Paul. Being able to argue comfortably with Paul was one of the things that Natalie liked about their relationship. He was like her father, that way; he listened to what she said, took her seriously, and encouraged her to stick to what she believed, even if he didn't agree with her. Most of the time.

But right now, Paul looked at her for a long time, frowned, and said, "Bullshit."

She had just told him, as she had told Becky and Gretchen that afternoon, about her desire to search for her natural parents. The girls had both said, "Why?"

Paul didn't ask why. He shook his head, and said again, "Bullshit."

They were sitting in his battered Volkswagen, in the driveway of the Armstrongs' house. They had been to a horror movie, and had laughed about it all the way home. The monsters had had visible seams and poorly synchronized eyes, and Paul had imitated a malfunctioning dinosaur as he drove. But the good humor had worn off when they began to talk.

"What do you mean by that?" Natalie was angry. She had expected Paul to understand.

"Nat," he said, "you have great parents, and you have no right to do that to them."

"My God, Paul, you're making me sound like some sort of a creep. I'm not doing anything to them. I *love* my parents. I just have to find out, that's all."

"Why? What difference does it make? None."

"That's easy for *you* to say. You know your ancestry all the way back to the *Mayflower*, practically. You have no idea how it feels not to know what your heritage is."

"Who cares? Natalie, I don't know who my ancestors are. It's all written down, and I've never read it. It doesn't matter to me. It only matters to my mother because she likes to go to those damn DAR conventions. Is that what you want, Nat, to put on a flowered hat and sing 'The Star-Spangled Banner'?"

"Cut it out, Paul. You know me better than that. Listen to me for a minute. I don't care about the distant past. I want to find my *mother*. I want to find out what happened, why I was born, why she gave me away. Who she was. Who she is."

He was silent for a minute. Then he said quietly, "And what if you found out she was a cheap whore working the Boston streets?"

Natalie felt as if he had slapped her. "You're rotten," she said.

"No, I'm not. I care about you, Nat. Listen, what a person *is* has nothing to do with where they come from, not with what *body* they come from."

"That's not true."

Paul sighed. "Natalie, do you remember Brenda whats-her-name, the girl who dropped out of school in tenth grade?"

Natalie looked at him. "Yes," she said. "She flunked every course, even cooking. But she had that nice smile. I remember her smile, always kind of dumb and puzzled and scared. Lonely. Why?"

"Well, Brenda works down at the fish factory now. She still has that same smile — lonely, dumb. Maybe that's why, the loneliness, the dumbness. Brenda goes to bed with anyone who smiles back and buys her two beers."

"So?"

"So. Suppose I went down to the waterfront after I leave here tonight, bought Brenda a couple of beers, and screwed her."

16

"*Paul*."

"I'm not going to, Nat. But I *could*. Half the guys in the senior class *have*. Now, suppose I did, and suppose Brenda became pregnant, with my child. She wouldn't even know it was mine. It could be anyone's. Suppose she gave birth to that child, out of her skinny, scared, borderline-retarded body. Do you think that baby would have anything to do with me?"

"Yes," said Natalie. "It might have your eyes. Your intelligence. It would be very much a part of you."

"Well, that's bullshit, Nat," Paul said angrily. "I don't believe that. It would be a baby, that's all. Probably sickly. Born by mistake, because someone was horny and had a couple of bucks to spend on beer. 'Heritage' is a meaningless word."

"Let me ask you something, Paul. Do you think that I could have been born to a prostitute — or, as you put it, a cheap whore working the Boston streets? Or to some vacant-brained person like Brenda?"

He looked away, out of the car window, across the lawn, and didn't answer.

"*Do* you?" she asked again.

"No," he said, finally.

"Well, I don't either, damn it. I think that *somewhere* there is a dark-haired woman who, for whatever reasons, gave birth to a baby girl whom she couldn't keep. And that she still thinks about it, and wonders where that baby is. Where *I* am. And I'm going to find her, Paul. I have a right to."

She kissed him quickly and got out of the car. He started the engine, and called to her. "Nat?"

"What?" She went to the window on his side.

"Don't hurt your parents."

She stood there silently, hugging her arms around her in the spring night breeze. "I already have," she said. "I wish that weren't part of it." Then she turned and ran across the lawn to the porch, as he backed his car from the driveway and headed home.

"NATALIE," said her father. "We *haven't* just forgotten about it. Your mother and I have talked and talked."

"Why haven't you talked to *me?*"

"We will, Natalie. Give us time. It's not an easy thing."

"It isn't for me, either."

"I know, sweetheart," he said. "Just give us some more time." He hugged her.

I love this man, she thought. My father. Why isn't that enough?

NANCY CAME into her room and closed the door. "Nat," she asked, "what's with you and the rents?"

Natalie groaned. "Nancy, why do you have to talk in that ridiculous super-teen-ager-abbreviated way? The word is 'Parents.'"

Nancy grinned. "Okay. What's with you and the parents?

Natalie was brushing her hair. "What do you mean?" she asked.

"Hey, let me fool with your hair, okay? How are you going to wear it at graduation?" Nancy took the brush, collected her sister's heavy dark hair in her hands, and made a chignon on the top of Natalie's head. "Hey, not bad. Not bad."

Natalie looked in the mirror as Nancy held the mound of hair carefully in place. "Yeah, I kind of like that, Nance. But it wouldn't work. I have to wear one of those stupid flat hats at graduation. Move it down a little."

Nancy rearranged the bundle of hair lower, at Natalie's neck. It made her look older, more sophisticated. They stared at their paired images in the mirror. Nancy's hair was light, curly, and short: the kind of hair that always looked the same, no matter how she tried to re-do it. She pouted at herself, making her dimples appear, and she crossed her eyes and giggled. Then she released Natalie's hair so that it fell thick and straight again. "You're so lucky," she said to her sister.

I wish people would stop telling me I'm lucky, thought Natalie. Or else that I would feel lucky, or that I believed being lucky is a good thing.

"I drank two beers at Karen's party Saturday night," confided Nancy. "Then I threw up."

"Taught you a lesson," said Natalie.

"Yeah. Taught me to get to the bathroom faster. I threw up on their kitchen floor. It was gross. No one would help me clean it up."

"Dad has told you a hundred times that if you're going to drink, at least drink very slowly. Space it out. How fast did you drink two beers?"

"About five minutes. It was a contest. I won. But the win was declared illegal because I threw up."

"Did you tell Dad?"

Nancy laughed. "I didn't have to. He was up when I came home. He said my face was the color of Furacin Gauze. What color is Furacin Gauze?"

"Sort of vomity yellow."

"I figured. I don't know how you stand working in his office. Yuck."

"I used to be grossed out, sometimes. But you get used to it. And Dad's good to work for. He told me when I started that I would have to look at everything. Not to turn away. If you have to faint or throw up, he said, go in another room and do it. But don't avoid anything, because you're going to have to see it all, someday. It's part of what life is, he said. And if I really wanted to be a doctor, I would have to learn to deal with all of it."

"Did you, ever? Faint, or throw up?"

"No. I cried, once."

"Why?"

"Well, it's kind of a long story. It was early last summer. One of those days when the office had been filled with people all day long. It was about five o'clock, and there were still patients in most of the examining rooms, waiting. The receptionist was getting one phone call after another. Dad and the nurse were in one of the examining rooms, and I was in the lab washing instruments, when the receptionist came in, all hassled, and said she absolutely *had* to go to the bathroom, and could I please sit at her desk for a few minutes.

"So I took her place, and the minute she was gone, a young couple came running into the office, holding a baby wrapped in a blanket. The mother was screaming something about the baby, and the father was talking, trying to explain, and they handed it to me and said, 'Do something!' They just shoved it into my arms, both of them talking and crying.

"Well, I ran down the hall with the baby. The parents came behind me, and Dad's office door was open. I told them to go in there and sit down. Then I banged on the door of the room where Dad was with a patient, and told him to come to the third examining room right away, and I took the baby in there and laid it on the table. Dad came right behind me, but I knew the baby was dead before he got there. It was just — well, it was dead, that's all.

"He began doing things very fast, but then he just slowed down and stopped and looked very tired. He said the baby had been dead for several hours, and asked me where the parents were, and if they had said anything.

"I told him they were waiting in his office, that they had just screamed at me something about the baby not waking up from his nap, and when they went in to get him, he was this way, all still and pale. Dad took the little nightgown and shirt off the baby, and examined him very carefully, but there wasn't a mark on him.

"Finally, Dad said, 'Natalie, this looks like a case of what we call Sudden Infant Death Syndrome. There's no explanation for it; it just happens, and for some reason it happens mostly to male infants this age. There will have to be an autopsy, of course. I can't do anything for this baby. But the parents need me, and I'm going to have to go to be with them, now.'

"Then he saw that I had started to cry. He became very stern. He said, 'Stop it, Natalie. Stop it, *right now*.' He told me again that he was going to the parents, and that he wanted me to stay with the baby. He told me to dress it carefully, and to comb its hair, so that when its parents saw it, it wouldn't be lying naked on an examining table like a medical specimen.

"Then he left me there. I stopped crying. I made a fresh diaper out of an examining room towel, because his diaper was wet. I pinned it on with the pins from his wet diaper, little pins with blue plastic tops shaped like ducks' heads. I put on his little undershirt, and the blue and white checked nightie he'd been wearing. I washed his face. Then I combed his hair. He had dark hair, and I combed it the way I thought his mother probably did, so that it curled at the top of his head. And — you want to know something crazy, Nance?"

Nancy nodded.

"I talked to him while I was doing it. He just seemed so alone, lying there, all still that way. I said, 'You're a lovely little boy. You didn't have a very long life, but I bet it was a good one. I bet you smiled at your mother when she rocked you. Now I want you to look very beautiful when your mom and dad say goodbye to you.' And I curled his hair around my fingers, so that he did, he looked beautiful.

"After a while Dad came in, with the parents, and I left

them there. Dad had called the hospital, and someone came to pick them up. They went out of the back door. The father was carrying the baby's body.

"Dad came into the lab where I was, and took me into his office, and closed the door. 'Now,' he said, 'cry.' And I did. I sobbed and sobbed, and he sat there with his arms around me. And when finally I stopped crying and blew my nose, he said, 'Natalie, you are going to be a very good doctor someday.'"

Nancy sat silently, staring at her sister. "I couldn't have done it, Nat. I couldn't even have *looked* at a dead baby."

"Yes, you could," said Natalie. "You can do anything, if you have to."

"Only knock off the booze, okay?"

Nancy grinned. "You sound like Mom."

"Look," said Natalie. "You asked what was with me and the — ah, the rents? Read this, and tell me how you feel."

She gave Nancy the sheet of paper from the desk drawer. Nancy curled up in the wicker chair and read it over.

"I think," she said slowly, when she'd finished, "that if it were *me*, I wouldn't care one way or another. But I think also that it isn't me, it's you. If it means that much to you, I'll help you however I can."

"Thanks, Nance. I think it's something I have to do alone. But I'm glad you understand."

"There's one thing I can do," Nancy said.

"What?"

"I'll talk to Mom and Dad."

6 BECKY AND GRETCHEN knocked on the back door and came into the kitchen as Natalie was having a Saturday morning cup of coffee with her mother. The kitchen sink was filled with bright yellow dandelion blossoms.

"Bleccch," said Becky, making a face. "What're *those* for?"

Natalie looked archly at her mother. "You might as well tell them, Mom."

Kay Armstrong looked slightly embarrassed. "Well," she said. Then she poured herself some more coffee. "Want some?" They shook their heads.

"Well," she said, again. "I decided I would make some dandelion wine."

"Hey," said Gretchen. "That's neat. How do you make it?"

Kay Armstrong didn't say anything.

"Tell them all of it, Mom." Natalie laughed.

"I don't know how to make it," she confessed. "Let me start at the beginning. Last night, when I was just about to fall asleep — you know how you get these *great* ideas when you're just about to fall asleep? — it occurred to me that it would be terrific to make dandelion wine. Have either of you ever tasted dandelion wine?"

They shook their heads.

"Neither have I," said Kay Armstrong. "Nevertheless, it seemed like a marvelous fun thing to do, last night. But I remembered that there aren't any dandelions in our yard. Natalie's father is a fantastic gardener. Every spring he does magic things to the lawn, so that there are no broad-leafed weeds. That includes dandelions. Have you ever noticed that we have no broad-leafed weeds in our yard?"

Becky and Gretchen giggled. "No," they said.

"Well, take a look, when you go out. No broad-leafed weeds. Anyway, as I was lying there half-asleep, I remembered that the neighbors two doors away, the Gibsons, have terrible dandelions. Millions. Obviously they haven't conquered the broad-leafed weed problem. So I decided to use the Gibsons' dandelions.

"But the Gibsons are away this weekend. Their daughter is being married in Denver. No way to call and ask their permission."

She took another sip of coffee. "So I decided to steal their dandelions. I thought I would do it very early in the morning, when no one would see me in their yard.

"So I set my mental alarm clock for five o'clock. Do you girls know how to set a mental alarm clock?"

They shook their heads.

"Well, that's a different subject, but I'll tell you about it sometime. It has to do with self-hypnosis. Anyway, five o'clock came, and I woke up, and got out of bed very quietly, because I didn't want Alden to know what I was doing, in case he would have thought I was quite mad. Do *you* think I'm quite mad?"

"No," said Becky.

"Yes," said Natalie.

"Well, he half woke up anyway, and said, with his eyes closed, 'What time is it? Where are you going?' and I said, 'It's five o'clock, and I'm going to the bathroom,' and *he* said, 'You should have your kidneys x-rayed,' and then he turned over and was sound asleep again, and I got my bathrobe and went downstairs.

"I went over to the Gibsons' yard, through the O'Haras' back yard, wearing my bathrobe, and when I got there and stood in the middle of all those dandelions . . . it was a great feeling, incidentally; the sun was just coming up, and the grass was damp, and their yard is bright yellow, it has so many dandelions; it was really exhilarating . . . I realized I had nothing to put the dandelions in.

"So I took off my bathrobe and put it on the ground and began to fill it with dandelion blossoms. The whole thing was really lovely. I was wearing a white nightgown, and I think I must have looked like a painting by Renoir, bending over and picking flowers in the sunrise. It's a *beautiful* nightgown, by the way; would you call it translucent, Natalie?"

"No. Transparent."

"Perhaps. Well, there was no one around. So I filled up my bathrobe, and pulled the corners together and tied them, so that it was a nice bundle, and *then* it occurred to me to try balancing it on my head, you know, the way native women do in the South Seas?"

Becky and Gretchen were hysterical.

"Don't laugh." Kay Armstrong grinned. "I walked back home, through the O'Haras' yard, very carefully, with my bathrobe full of dandelion blossoms on my head. It was a nice exercise in posture, I think. Anyway, that's what I was doing when the milkman drove into our driveway and met me.

"I started to explain to him what I was doing, but I confess that I became a little embarrassed, because I was aware that my nightgown was *slightly* indecent, although I *do* think I'd call it translucent, Natalie —

"And of course I couldn't put my bathrobe on, because it was filled with dandelions —"

"And on your head," interrupted Gretchen.

"Don't be silly. Of course I took it off my head when I saw the milkman.

"I could see that he didn't have the slightest idea what I was talking about, so I thought I would just go into the house pleasantly without any further conversation. And I said, 'Have a nice day' to the milkman, and started to open the back door, but I had locked myself out.

"I had to ring the bell quite a while before Alden woke up and came down, and in the meantime the milkman didn't know whether to go or stay, so he stayed, and when Alden appeared at the door, there I was in my nightgown, holding my bundle of dandelions, and the milkman standing there looking stricken, as if he had walked into a lunatic asylum by mistake."

"What did Dr. Armstrong say?" asked Becky.

"He just stood there for a minute, and then finally said, 'Didn't you have to go to the bathroom?' The milkman fled." Kay Armstrong dissolved in laughter.

"Then later," she said, "I realized that I haven't any idea how to make dandelion wine. It didn't even seem a good idea, anymore. So I put all the dandelions in the sink, and two bumblebees flew out and stung me on the arm, which made me feel that the dandelions are decidedly hostile to the whole thing as well, and *now* —" she got up, went to the sink, and pressed a switch — "I am sending them all down the garbage disposal."

"'*Sic transit gloria.*'" Gretchen laughed.

"What does that mean?" asked Becky.

"It means I'm going to be sick, gloriously, from laughing."

"Nat," said Becky seriously, when they were in Natalie's bedroom later, "how can you not be satisfied with your mother?"

"I am," said Natalie. "It has nothing to do with that at all."

7   GRADUATION DAY was like every other Graduation Day. She had attended them for several years, had watched her friends stand there on the stage in their caps and gowns, the girls holding red roses, some of the kids collecting their awards, some of them wearing the special stoles that indicated particular honors. The school band, heavy on clarinets, playing the school song; the tears and smiles; the traditional flipping of tassels from one side to the other. The proud parents with their flashcubes popping. The speeches: they were the same, really, every year.

But because it was her graduation, because it was her father carefully focusing his camera to get what she knew from experience would be blurred snapshots of decapitated people, Natalie listened to the nervous voices of the three students chosen to speak, and tried to attach some meaning in their words to her own life.

Gretchen was one of the speakers. Her high grades had consistently led the class for years, and she had won the scholarships that would take her to Wellesley to study political science. Natalie grinned when Gretchen rose to speak, knowing that under the heavy graduation gown, her friend was wearing patched and faded denim shorts. It was a hot day; summer had really come, and was welcome.

"Commencement," Gretchen began, "means Beginning." Some of the students glanced at each other, and smiled. How many graduation speeches had started, "Commencement means Beginning"?

Natalie found her family in the crowd. Her father was solemn and attentive, wearing his best suit, and for once the ends of his stethoscope were not protruding from his breast pocket. Nancy was beside him, her hair curlier than usual from the humidity of the early June afternoon, her blue eyes darting here and there as she searched in the audience for her friends. Nancy wasn't listening, Natalie knew. It didn't matter, she thought. Next year, when Nancy graduates, someone will stand up here and say the same thing again: "Commencement means Beginning." Her mother, her face youthful and attractive, was listening, but she was watching Natalie, not Gretchen. Nat caught her eye and they winked at each other and grinned.

The Branford High School gym looked more austere than it ordinarily did. During basketball season, there was usually a huge, clumsily lettered sign that said "Be an Athletic Supporter" taped to the wall behind the far basket. That was gone. For the senior prom in May, the gym had been transformed by dim light, crepe-paper streamers, a mirrored revolving ball hanging from the center of the ceiling to catch the colored lights, and tables covered with pastel cloths had been arranged around the sides of the room. All those one-night bits of magic were gone, too.

So it was just a gym. Still, it seemed awesome, the whole atmosphere of graduation.

"But there are beginnings, perhaps," Gretchen was saying slowly, "that shouldn't be made at all." Natalie watched her and listened more closely.

"We must examine our own motives. Might we be embarking on quests beyond our capacity for understanding?

"We have become complacent here, as seniors. We've been the school leaders — the guys who know it all, have done it all. We're old enough now to be on our own. Some of us will be going to college, some off to full-time jobs, some to be married —" the graduates all grinned at Marcia Pickering, who blushed and polished her tiny diamond ring with one finger — "and to be honest, we, all of us, think we're pretty hot stuff right now.

"But we're very young. We shouldn't forget that. We shouldn't forget that there are doors not ready to be opened. That if we choose certain paths we may be unhappily surprised by where they lead. And we shouldn't forget that those who have helped and advised us till now — our parents, teachers, and others — are still here to give help, and advice, and, when we need it, sympathy and understanding.

"Most of you remember the movie *Bambi*. How Bambi stood at the edge of the forest and was frightened of the big, open meadow, as he had every reason to be. There were dangers there.

"We will all have to go into the dangerous and unknown places that await us. But we should be careful not to rush, not to move ahead without thinking. We should save each beginning until we are prepared to face everything it leads to

"If we do, each Commencement after this one will bring growth and meaning to our lives.

"Thank you."

Gretchen sat down, embarrassed by the applause, grateful to be finished. Natalie looked over at her, caught her eye, smiled, and gave her a thumbs-up sign.

Then the speeches were ended, the diplomas awarded, the tassels flipped, the school band prodded by the music director into a final march, and the graduates moved in double rows down the aisle and out of the wide door at the entrance to the gym. Natalie found her family in the crowd. She gave her rose to Nancy, hugged her parents, and threw a kiss across the front lawn to Paul, who was standing sheepishly in front of his father's Instamatic camera, saying "Cheese."

"Let's go home!" urged Nancy.

"Oh, wait, I want to see all my friends," said Natalie.

"Nat, let's go home. There are *presents*," said Nancy.

Natalie laughed. Nancy was still, at sixteen, awake before dawn on Christmas morning; Nancy still said the word "presents" with all the uninhibited glee of a four-year-old — even if the presents weren't for her, and that was one of the nice things about Nancy.

She opened the gifts in the living room at home, and her mother took the ribbons as she unwrapped the packages, one by one, and arranged them on Natalie's head. By the third she was festooned with curled-ended bows, yellow, green, and pink, and felt like the Alice in Wonderland illustration of the Dutchess' baby in its huge ruffled cap. She felt self-indulgent and silly, as if she had been sipping champagne.

From Nancy, there was a fragile silver necklace, a small shining knot caught at the end of a smooth-linked chain. She held it over her hands and remembered how, as a child, she had tried once to capture a small waterfall, in vain. Then she fastened the clasp at the back of her neck and smiled at her sister.

Aunt Helen was on a Mediterranean cruise; she had sent a package. All four of them found themselves glancing inadvertently at the top of the television. The package was too small to be another panther.

"I could save it till last," Natalie suggested.

"No, get it over with," said Nancy practically. "Save Mom and Dad's till last."

"I wonder if it's membership in the exotic-fruit-of-the-month club," said Natalie's mother, remembering a year when they had dutifully unpacked, month after month, unidentifiable squishy, semi-rotted sweet-smelling things that they had pondered and then sent down the disposal.

"Hey!" said Natalie in pleased surprise, holding it up. "Look!" It was a leather-bound medical dictionary.

Her father exhaled in startled relief. "She's mellowed," he said. "At last."

Kay Armstrong chuckled. "Like the mango?" she said. The mango, indeed, had mellowed. It had mellowed all over the inside of the box in which it had been packed, during its month as exotic fruit, and had dripped, as they carried it, noses averted, to the sink.

"No," said Natalie. "Aunt Helen's okay." She opened the cover of the book and read the inscription that her father's sister had written. She grimaced. "Well, she's semi-okay."

"Semi-Horrible Aunt Helen," said Nancy. "What did she write?"

"Just one of her pronouncements," Natalie said. "Are you sure you want to hear it?"

"No," said her father. "But read it anyway."

Natalie stood, faced them, and tried to assume Aunt Helen's pinched-mouth voice. "'It is not a field for a woman,' she read, 'but since you have chose Medicine, you have my wishes for success.'"

They all sighed. "You're right, Nancy," said Dr. Armstrong. "She's my sister, but she's semi-horrible."

"Like a semipermeable membrane," suggested Natalie's mother. "Some things get through. But not enough. Well, it's a nice dictionary."

("Well," she had said once, "it's the *nicest* green ceramic panther I've ever seen. I'll give it that.")

"Open Tallie's," said Nancy impatiently. "Open Tallie's."

They said it every Christmas, every birthday: open Tallie's, open Tallie's.

Tallie Chandler was Natalie's only living grandparent. The sculptor, her mother's mother, lived in a Boston apartment in the winter, and spent her summers on an island off the coast of Maine. By car and boat, she was only five hours away; but there was nothing, not even a granddaughter's graduation, that would take her from Ox Island. "She came to our wedding," Kay Armstrong had explained once, laughing, "but only because we scheduled it for the weekend before she was leaving Boston, and we had it at her apartment."

The package was heavy. Underneath its outer wrappings, the box was wrapped in off-white tissue paper that had been block-printed with an abstract design in blue and green.

"She's incredible," murmured Dr. Armstrong. "Look at that, Kay. She did that paper by hand. She should have signed it. You could frame it, if it weren't folded and wrinkled."

Kay Armstrong smiled. "When I was a little girl," she mused, remembering, "every meal we had — *every* meal — looked like a still life that should have a frame around it. I remember once, when I was very small, watching her arranging breakfast on four plates. We were in Italy at the time, and there was a guest at the house; I forget who. And I asked her why she was taking so long. I was *hungry*. She laughed, and said she was just perfecting the symmetry before she served it."

"*Open* it," said Nancy.

Natalie set the paper aside carefully and opened the box. She gasped.

It was a small, gleaming, perfectly cast piece of bronze sculpture. It was abstract, but there was all of nature in it. It could have been a gull at sunrise, motionless, with its head caught, bent, in the fold of a wing; it could have been the thick, unopened leaves of a deep-forest wild plant in early spring. Natalie turned it gently in her hands, and it caught the sun. In the base, Tallie had etched her signature.

A small white card had fallen from the box. Natalie picked it up and read aloud, "Natalie dearest. I have titled this piece 'Commencement,' and I created it with my namesake in mind. May it bring you joy. May all Commencements bring you joy. Tallie."

"You know," said Dr. Armstrong after a moment, "that's worth a fortune."

Natalie held the sculpture and stroked its perfect curved lines with her hand. "It would be worth a fortune," she said, "even if it weren't worth a fortune."

She set it on the coffee table so that the sun, coming through the west windows of the room, enlarged its shadow into a curved image on the polished pine.

"Now I'll open yours." She smiled at her parents.

Their gift was a small box. When Natalie removed the paper, she saw the department store label on the cardboard box, and some familiar Scotch-tape marks on the sides. "*Mom*," she said. "This is the same box that held the necktie I gave Dad on Father's Day!"

"Well," her mother laughed. "Don't knock it. Recycling is environmentally sound."

Inside the box was simply a thin stack of papers tied with a ribbon. On top of the tied packet lay a folded sheet of stationery. She opened it, puzzled, and read the letter that was typed on her father's office letterhead.

*

Our dearest Natalie,

This gift is from your mother and me, with all our love. And it is from Nancy, who persuaded us that it was what you deserved to have.

We will give you the summer — this summer of your graduation — to make the search you want to make for your own past.

The box contains all the documents we have. They are very few, and your search, I'm afraid, will be a difficult and perhaps a painful one.

Your job at my office begins, as you know, next Monday. I need your help there, and I think you need the experience there to make your choice of a profession a reasoned and meaningful one. But I have scheduled your work this summer to run only through each Thursday at noon. So you will have three and a half days of each weekend to do whatever you must.

I have opened a checking account in your name and placed enough money there to make possible whatever traveling you will find necessary. The checkbook is also in the box.

You will find, also, a set of keys. I have leased a car for your use this summer as well.

You are mature, sensitive, and responsible. We wish you success in whatever journeys you make in these next three months. But we want you to know, also, that what you find is not important to us. You are our daughter, and our friend as well. We love you for being Natalie, and that's all that matters to us.

Both of her parents had signed the letter. Natalie was crying by the time she read their signatures. She folded the paper again, took the bouquet of bright ribbons from her hair, and hugged them.

"Thank you," she said. "Thank you."

Then she whispered also, "I'm sorry."

8	MUCH LATER, in her room alone, Natalie opened the box again. She felt curiously frightened. It was what she had wanted; now, holding the clues to her own past in her hands, she felt uncertain. Paul

had said, "Why bother? The present is enough. Today is enough." And perhaps it was, after all. Tallie's sculpture sat on her desk like a symbol of an unopened tomorrow — a commencement — surrounded by the simple, unobstructed lines of today. There seemed none of yesterday's secrets in the bronze.

But she wanted the yesterdays, though she feared them. She felt as she had, years before, on her first day of school, clutching the security of her mother's firm hand, terrified, puzzled, not knowing if she would like what she found in this new world, not knowing if it would like her. Still, she had finally pushed her mother's hand away, then, and whispered, "Go on. I'm okay." As once her father had left her alone in an examining room, with things that had filled her with fear and pain.

She unfolded the first paper. It was, as the letter had been, typed by her father on his office stationery.

To Whom It May Concern:
    My adopted daughter, Natalie C. Armstrong (*no*, thought Natalie. You have always called me "*My daughter*") is undertaking to investigate her natural parentage. She is doing this with the permission and understanding of myself and of her mother.
    I would appreciate your cooperation in providing her with any helpful information that might be available to you.

Sincerely,
Alden T. Armstrong, M.D.

The next paper was obviously older. It was marred at its borders by torn places, and the edges were discolored. It was dated July 10, 1960. Two months before I was born, thought Natalie.

The letterhead was oddly familiar. Harvey, Mac-Pherson, and Lyons, Attorneys at Law, Branford, Maine. Hal MacPherson was her father's lawyer; the MacPhersons were family friends. They lived two blocks away; Natalie had dated their son a couple of times when he was home on college vacations. What had the Mac-Phersons to do with her birth? It was disquieting, that all these years, perhaps, the MacPhersons had known something of Natalie that she herself had not known. Not fair. Of course, the fact that she had been adopted had never been a secret. But the MacPhersons? She had always called him Uncle Hal, affectionately. And he had known more of her than she had been permitted to know? Why am I angry? Natalie thought. Is this what Dad meant when he said the search would be a painful one? She smoothed the letter with her hands and began to read.

HARVEY, MACPHERSON, AND LYONS,
ATTORNEYS AT LAW
30 Bay Street, Branford, Maine

102 Caldwell Avenue   *July 10, 1960*
Branford, Maine

Dear Alden:

Please forgive me if I am intruding in a personal matter. But Pat, my wife, is a friend of Kay's, and she has been aware of the difficulties you and Kay have encountered in dealing with the state adoption agency.

Although you and I don't know each other well, I am certainly familiar with your reputation professionally as well as through the community services that you have contributed to Branford since you have come here. If I can be of service to you in regard to the process of adoption, I would like to offer my availability.

I don't know how familiar you are with the process of so-called private adoptions. This is a term, as you perhaps know, applied to those adoptions arranged without going through the official procedures of an agency. There are very often disadvantages to private adoptions; notably, the lack of extensive screening and matching procedures that agencies provide.

On the other hand, there are particular advantages in the case of people like Kay and yourself, for whom agency procedures have become long and frustrating. I would be happy to meet with you and your wife to discuss the pros and cons of private adoption if you would like.

But I am writing this letter because it has recently been brought to my attention, through a lawyer in the northern part of the state, to whom I was talking recently about different matters, that a child will be born shortly — I believe this fall — whose family has sought his advice about private adoption placement. I know nothing about how much importance to place on genetics in such a circumstance; you, as a physician, are much more qualified to deal with that question than I. But the lawyer that I mentioned seemed to find that a matter of concern, and mentioned that this particular infant will be born to parents of substantial intelligence and good health.

If you and Kay would like to talk about this further, please feel free to call me at my office. If it is something that does not interest you, I will understand, and hope, as I said, that you will forgive the intrusion.

In the meantime, let me take this opportunity to congratulate you on the presentation that you made the other night at the meeting of the Medical-Legal Committee of the Bar Association. A fine job; Branford is indeed fortunate to have you in our midst.

> Very Sincerely,
>
> Harold MacPherson

Natalie sat on the edge of her bed, read the letter again, and saw that her hands were shaking.

A child will be born shortly. That was me. He wrote about it as if he could have as easily been saying, "A new car will be delivered when the next shipment arrives."

To parents of "substantial intelligence and good health." She laughed briefly, and with no humor, to herself. Well, that lets out Fish-Factory Brenda, or her equivalent. I'm glad of *that*, anyway.

Why am I not very glad about the rest of it?

She lay back on her bed, crossed her hands behind her head, and watched the ceiling of her bedroom where the first car headlights of early evening were crossing it occasionally in patterns that formed, moved, disappeared, and formed again.

It's because it was all so *cold*. "A child." My God. If I had been conceived by my parents, they would have been thinking in terms of "our baby." Not "a child." But here, the very first time I appear on the scene, it's in a letter written by a lawyer — maybe by his secretary — as if I were a pending transaction!

Someone, though, thought Natalie, was thinking of me as "my baby." Great. And hating the idea of me so much that they were already deciding to give me away! She looked at the letter again. "Have sought his advice about private adoption placement."

In her mind, she formed a picture, like a scene in a movie, of a couple sitting in a lawyer's office. The woman pregnant. I was born in September; this letter is dated July. She was very visibly pregnant when she went to this lawyer and said . . . what? "I am seeking your advice about private adoption placement"? Or: "Listen, I don't want to keep this kid"?

Was there a man with her? The letter says "family." Maybe there were children already. Maybe I had brothers and sisters. Maybe they went to the lawyer and said, "Hey, we didn't intend to have another baby, and now here we are, the wife is pregnant, and we just can't afford another child."

Abortion was not legal seventeen years ago. Had they considered it, anyway?

Another picture formed, briefly, and she liked this one a little better. The woman was pregnant, weeping, and beautiful. Her husband held her hand in the lawyer's office, and explained sadly, "My wife has an incurable disease. She has only a year to live. I can't raise a child alone. So we want you to find a home for our child."

But that was romantic and foolish, she knew; the letter had said "substantial intelligence and good health." Natalie closed her eyes and let the flickering scenes of her imagination drift away as if they were lights moving across the ceiling. Nothing replaced them except emptiness; emptiness diffused by disappointment, pain, and an anger that she couldn't understand. Finally she sat up, turned on the light against the increasing darkness, and took the next paper from the box.

PEABODY AND GOODWIN, ATTORNEYS AT LAW
SIMMONS' MILLS, MAINE

102 Caldwell Avenue   *July 25, 1960*
Branford, Maine

Dear Dr. and Mrs. Armstrong:

Hal MacPherson has written me of your interest in the child which I have been authorized to place for adoption. He speaks very highly of you as potential parents for this child, and I am delighted to be able to let you know that I see no possible barriers at this point to the adoption taking place.

Let me fill you in to the extent that I am able on the details of the case.

The child will be born in September. The family was referred to me by Dr. Clarence Therrian, a general practitioner in Simmons' Mills, who has been handling the medical aspects of the mother's pregnancy.

For your protection and for that of the child, Dr. Therrian and I have investigated the background as thoroughly as possible. Naturally, any specific information about the parentage remains confidential. But I am authorized to tell you that there are no familial diseases on the side of either parent. The general health and intelligence of both parents are substantially above average. The mother is of medium height and weight, with dark brown hair and blue eyes. The father is tall and slender, with brown hair and eyes; he is exceptionally well coordinated, with a great deal of athletic skill.

That is all official information. I will add, unofficially, that I know both parents personally, and feel certain that their combined attributes will bring to this child an unusual combination of attractive characteristics. I have no hesitancy about recommending this as an exceptionally good adoptive risk.

Let me tell you briefly what the adoptive procedure involves. At some point in the next month or so, Hal MacPherson will have you fill out the necessary Petition for Adoption form. He will send it along to me. After the birth has taken place, I will have the mother sign the second page, and the petition will then go to a probate judge. Since you have already been investigated and approved by the state agency, there is no reason to suspect that he would not readily grant the petition.

The Bureau of Vital Statistics will issue an amended birth certificate, naming you as parents, and the original birth certificate will be sealed by the court.

I must remind and warn you of two things.

The mother, until she signs the petition after the birth of the child, is free to change her mind about the adoption. I do not believe she will do so. Nevertheless I would be remiss in not alerting you to the fact that it would be her privilege, and that there have been cases in which the natural mother has had such a change of heart after the child has been born.

Secondly, the name of the natural parents will not be made known to you, nor yours to them. Hal MacPherson will not know the names of the parents, and Dr. Therrian will not know your names. I will be the only party who knows the names of both involved parties, and I feel very strongly about not divulging that information.

If you have made your decision, I would appreciate it if you would get together with Hal and sign your part of the Petition for Adoption, so that he can send it along to me. I look forward to notifying you in September when the birth has taken place, and I take this opportunity to wish you great happiness.

Sincerely,
Foster H. Goodwin

The final paper in the small box, resting on top of the car keys and checkbook, was a folded yellow telegram.

PETITION HAS BEEN SIGNED AUTHORIZING ADOPTION OF SIX POUND EIGHT OUNCE HEALTHY BABY GIRL BORN FOUR THIRTY AM SEPTEMBER FOURTEENTH. PLEASE BE AT MY OFFICE 43 MAIN STREET SIMMONS' MILLS 2 PM SEPTEMBER NINETEENTH AND I WILL GIVE YOU YOUR DAUGHTER. CONGRATULATIONS. FOSTER H. GOODWIN.

Natalie realized she was weeping, and that the anger had gone. Foster H. Goodwin, she thought, knew my real parents, and he liked them. I can tell that, even though he didn't say it. And even though he talked of "the child" and "the birth," which set my teeth on edge, he only did it because he had to. And when I was born . . . (at FOUR THIRTY AM SEPTEMBER FOURTEENTH, she thought, grinning through the warm tears on her face) . . . he was thrilled, and happy for my parents. And he said "your daughter" to Mom and Dad.

This isn't going to be hard, after all. Even though he said he felt strongly about not divulging the information, he's a kind man, and I can make him change his mind.

Natalie looked through the bookcase in her room until she found the large United States atlas that, she realized with a smile, Aunt Helen had given her one Christmas when she would much rather have had a new sweater.

The map of Maine was on page 32. She tilted the

lampshade so that the full light of the bulb fell on the page, and searched the state for Simmons' Mills. Finally she found it; the name jumped out at her from a space in the north-central mountainous section of the state, and she held her finger there and looked at it for a long time. The small circle with a dot in the center, there on the edge of the Penobscot River, was keyed to indicate that Simmons' Mills had a population between 1000 and 2500.

"Oh, I'm just a small-town girl," she announced aloud, giggling to herself.

She followed with her finger the route she would take from Branford. Main highways as far as Bangor; beyond that, to the north, it would be increasingly smaller, more curving roads, through the mountains, along the river, to the town where she was born. The town where she would find Foster H. Goodwin and, through him, her real parents.

Then her eyes slid to the coast, and she saw Ox Island, a tiny dark blue dot in the lighter blue of Frenchman's Bay.

First, thought Natalie, looking with joy at the sculpture that was now in shadows in the dark corner of the room where her desk was, I will go to see Tallie. Tallie has a way of putting everything in perspective, and before I set off on that long road that curves to a place called Simmons' Mills, I'll let my grandmother smoothe the edges of my questions into manageable shapes.

9 ON THE MAP, coastal Maine had the erratic pattern of cardiograms that Natalie had seen often in her father's office; it looked as if someone had taken a pen and drawn an irregular line, without looking, from New Hampshire to Canada at the edge of the Atlantic Ocean. The line moved, apparently aimlessly, in and out, forming peninsulas and promontories; it opened into harbors and coves where rivers arrived to empty into the sea.

Driving northeast on Route 1, Natalie was less aware of the random patterns of the coast. But she saw the ocean again and again on her right; she saw it curving around the edges of the small towns, the tide moving restlessly against the pilings that formed part of the docks and the fish-packing plants. It appeared in the desolate places that came now and then suddenly, after a bend in the road, where there were nothing but rocks and wind-sheared trees; and occasionally it was there against a short expanse of sand, where children would be playing with buckets and shovels and touching their toes into the icy water with shrieks of delighted pain.

It took her four hours to reach Northeast Harbor, a pleasant and uneventful drive in the small new car. The brilliant blue of the cove around which the little town clustered in a semicircle was spectacular. Northeast Harbor was a picture-postcard town; she could see the groups of tourists strolling the main street, their cameras dangling, their summer-vacation outfits so new the store creases were still visible. At the boat landing, she could pick out the ferries that took tourists to the bay islands on daily cruises. Natalie glanced down at her own faded jeans as she parked the car at the landing, and was devoutly glad that she was not wearing double-knit slacks, rhinestone-rimmed sunglasses, and driving a car with New York plates.

Snob, she thought, laughing at herself.

She lifted her backpack to her shoulders, pulled her hair loose from its webbed straps, and locked the car. Following the instructions Tallie had provided over the phone, she walked along the docks and looked for a small lobster boat named *Egret*. It was moored ignominiously behind a larger, more luxurious, cabin cruiser and moved up and down slowly as the water lifted it and let it go again.

Natalie looked down and waved at the man who sat on the boat with his legs up and a pipe in his mouth.

"Sonny?" She felt a little silly, but Tallie had told her someone named Sonny would be on the *Egret*.

"You the one goin' to Tallie's island?" he asked.

She smiled, nodded, and he reached up to help her aboard.

It wasn't Tallie's island. Natalie didn't know who owned the rest of it, but Tallie owned only four acres of Ox Island, which was two miles long and a half mile wide. It was typical of Tallie, though, thought Natalie, that people thought of it as Tallie's island.

It was typical, too, of a Maine lobsterman that he would have his jacket buttoned up tight against his chin in June, when the tourists were all in shirt-sleeves and alligator-adorned jerseys, and would be freezing and covered with goose bumps on the water. The breeze was very strong even before the *Egret* was out of the tight harbor, and downright cold as they crossed the open ocean to Ox Island.

"Do you know Tallie?" asked Natalie. "She's my grandmother."

Sonny was at the wheel, steering toward the island, watching the bay, not noticing the cold salt spray that struck his face as the boat moved.

"Yep," he said.

Natalie smiled to herself and didn't attempt any more conversation. If I were Tallie, she realized, I'd have him talking in long paragraphs, and before the fifteen-minute boat ride was over I'd know his life history.

Oh well, I'm not Tallie. No one is.

Sonny eased the boat gently toward the decaying dock at Ox Island. He muttered to himself, something about how they'd better fix that before the ice bust it up next winter, someone going to get hurt out here. When the boat was fast against the dock, he took Natalie's hand firmly and helped her up.

"You be here Sunday at two," he said roughly. "I'll take you back."

"Shall I pay you then?" she asked.

"She took care of it." He turned to his engine, ignoring her thank you.

Tallie wasn't at the dock. Natalie hadn't expected her to be. Tallie had never, according to Natalie's mother, been on time to anything in her life.

But she was at the house. Natalie walked up the dirt road, opened the never-locked door, and found her there, busy in the kitchen, singing "Un bel dì vedremo" from *Madama Butterfly*, loudly and slightly off-key, as she stirred something on the stove.

She looked up in surprise. "Natalie! Is it four o'clock

already? I *meant* to be at the dock to greet you! But one of the local fishermen stopped by this morning with the most wonderful gift of lobsters and scallops and halibut that I decided to make a paella . . . have you ever tasted paella, Natalie? Look, how the saffron changes ordinary rice to such a marvelous shade of gold! . . . and my goodness, I've lost track of the time. You look absolutely beautiful. I have always thought of you as a Modigliani person, and look . . . you've proven me correct by wearing your hair that way, so that it falls into those elongated lines. Are you hungry? Warm enough? In need of music? Let me put on some Bach, so that everything will seem orderly and precise."

Natalie shrugged off her backpack, laughing, because Tallie never changed; she was still the same; no matter what happened, Tallie would always be indescribable. She ran to her and hugged her, and they held each other for a long time.

10	THEY HAD TALKED and talked.

"Natalie," Tallie said at last, "even though you're certain that you want to — that you *have* to — make this search, you're frightened. Don't be. You can handle whatever you find. And of course one must find out everything. It's exactly what I would do myself. I've spent my life finding out everything I possibly can."

They were sitting, after supper, in the living room of Tallie's tiny, eighteenth-century farmhouse. It was, Natalie thought, her favorite room in the whole world. The past was in it, in the ancient pine boards of the floor, and in the small-paned windows with their interior shutters that had once been used to keep out unfriendly Indians, or, more often, the bitter winter wind. But the past was layered over by the present, and by Tallie's presence, in the form of the brilliant white paint with which she had painted the plaster walls, and over which she had hung vivid and abstract paintings. The hanging plants. The shaggy Danish rug in earth shades of brown and gray on the floor. The thick pottery ashtrays and bowls on the low tables. The bright woven pillows strewn at random on the low white couch. Everywhere, the books. And the music. Tallie's life was always filled with music. She had put a recording of noisy, quick Russian dances on her stereo; there were clapping and stamping combined with the abrupt and discordant melodies. Tallie had served tea on a tray: a murky tea to which she had added herbs that she had collected on the island and dried herself. She poured it from a rounded earthen pot into deep gold glazed-clay mugs. Natalie blew ripples into the surface of hers, and tested it with the tip of her tongue.

"But you know, Tallie," she said slowly, "Mom and Dad say they understand why I'm doing it, but they don't really. They're very hurt. And I'm not sure I understand myself, why I'm doing it."

"You have incredibly lovely feet, Natalie. You should *always* go barefoot. Of *course* they're hurt. Sometimes we have to hurt people, in order to keep ourselves whole. We must just do it with love, that's all."

"That doesn't make much sense to me," admitted Natalie.

"Where is it written that anything has to make sense? All I mean is that when you have to hurt someone you love, do it honestly. And you're doing that. You could have sneaked around and done what you're doing. It would have been more difficult, of course, but you could have done it, Natalie. And you didn't. You told them exactly what you were doing. And it hurt, but they know you love them."

"I bet you never hurt anyone, Tallie."

Tallie hooted with laughter, and reached for the pot to pour more tea. Her rings glittered in the soft light, and made small noises as the silver touched the thick pottery. "How do you think I *learned*? Of course I've hurt people. I ran away from my first husband in order to go off with your grandfather. You look shocked, Natalie. Didn't your mother ever tell you that?"

Natalie shook her head.

"Well, it's true. I lived in sin for quite a while before my first husband finally divorced me on grounds of adultery.

"Actually —" Tallie sipped her tea. "I lived in Italy." She chuckled. "Technically, it was in sin, at least according to my family and to the New York newspapers. But geographically, it was in Italy. That seemed the more important thing, since I couldn't speak a word of the language at first. Goodness; I wonder if there is a language for people who live in sin."

The music had ended, and the old farmhouse was very

quiet. A pale moth fluttered close to the small flame of the candle; the woman and the girl watched with vague amusement as the translucent wings drew it again and again to the potential danger. Finally Tallie caught the moth lightly with her quick hand, opened the window behind her, and released it to the night.

"They're so terribly fragile," she said. "I hope I didn't damage the wings. One tries so hard to save something, and sometimes things are injured in the saving."

She sighed. "It's the same thing we were talking about. I hurt people, by trying to save myself. Perhaps that was a brutal example. But there I was, twenty years old, madly in love with the most exciting man I'd ever met . . . have *still* ever met . . . and I was married to someone else. So what was I to do? Stay in New York the rest of my life, as the wife of a stockbroker who tucked his pajama tops carefully into the bottoms and wound his watch four times *exactly* every night before he went to bed?"

Natalie giggled.

"Or run off to Florence with an incredibly fine painter? Did I ever tell you how I met Stefan, Natalie? That he came over to my table in a New York restaurant and said, 'I want to paint you'? It sounds so trite, now; but nothing about Stefan was trite. Oh, Natalie, it was so exciting. And so *painful*.

"But there simply isn't any choice when you know you have to do something. So you inflict the hurt, and you smoothe it as much as you can by saying 'This is *my* fault, not yours — ' Your face is brightening. You said that, did you?"

Natalie nodded. "More or less."

"And it works out. You get through the pain, and it works out. In my case, I found incredible happiness. And my first husband married again, to a woman who was perfectly suited to him, who gave elegant dinner parties using the china he had inherited from his mother." She grimaced. "It was hideous, Natalie. Big green birds of paradise in the center of each plate; can you imagine? And they lived happily ever after. His obituary in the *New York Times* was twelve inches long, which surely would have pleased him; and it never mentioned that once, long ago, he had announced that he was going to jump out of his office window if I left. He did, Natalie, he said that as I was packing my bags, and all I could think of, even though I knew he would never really do it, was that he had always *abhorred* anything messy."

Natalie sipped more of her tea and smiled. "Well, Mom and Dad aren't *that* upset."

"Of course not. Your parents are sensible people. I'm being silly, dredging up my own insane past as an example. They'll get through it, and so will you, and you'll find your own past. If you like what you find, embrace it. If you don't, shrug it away."

Natalie curled into the corner of the wide couch, against the pile of bright cushions.

"Your mother used to do that when she was a little girl. Curl up into corners. I suppose it was because Stefan and I were forever taking her to places where we stayed longer than we thought we would. Sometimes *days* longer. Poor Katherine, we would find her curled in corners, fast asleep. Sometimes I think I was a bad mother." Tallie fitted a long cigarette into an even longer holder, and leaned forward to light it in the flame of the candle that still burned in its squat sculpted container on the table.

"Oh, you weren't, Tallie. I'm sure of it. Mom tells wonderful stories of her childhood."

Tallie smiled. "It's good having you here, Natalie. My Modigliani granddaughter. Do you think I look old?"

Her face was lined, and her hair was gray, but her eyes were dark and vivid, her mouth and hands alive and expressive. She was slender and small. "No," said Natalie honestly. "You don't even look old enough to be a grandmother, to me."

"Damn." Tallie laughed. "Thank you, I guess. But I am dying to be a fascinating old woman. Next year, perhaps."

She picked up the empty tea things and took them to the kitchen. "Let's go to bed now, Natalie," she called, "so that we can get up early tomorrow and have an all-day picnic. I'll take you to my favorite cove. How do you feel about going skinny-dipping in ice-cold water with an elderly friend?"

"I'll try anything once." Natalie laughed as she carried her backpack up the stairs.

 "I WISH I didn't have to go back," said Natalie sadly as she walked with Tallie to the boat landing on Sunday afternoon.

"Stay, then. We'll pick wild strawberries and make jam."

Natalie sighed. "I have to work tomorrow. Dad needs me. And the next free weekend I have —"

"You're going to go to that place — what was the funny name it had?"

"Simmons' Mills."

"Simmons' Mills. Yes. You'll find things there that will surprise you, Natalie. You're not afraid of them, are you?"

Natalie laughed uncertainly but she said, "No. I think they'll probably be very ordinary things. Nothing to be afraid of."

Sonny, still buttoned up in his salt-stiffened jacket, helped her into the rugged little boat. She reached up and held Tallie's hand tightly for a moment; then Sonny revved the engine and the boat moved gently from the dock.

Tallie had wrapped her arms around herself to shield her body from the chilly wind that was lifting foam from the murky and turbulent water of the bay. Natalie watched her grandmother diminish in size as the *Egret* carried them steadily apart, until Tallie was no more than a speck on the outlined edge of the island dock, and then she was nothing at all as light gray fog appeared and blurred the transition between sky, land, and sea.

Natalie felt the edges of her backpack to assure herself that the small box Tallie had given her was still safely there. "Open it later," Tallie had said, "when you have time, and solitude. I don't know if it will help at all. But it will add another dimension. In art, it's important to find all the dimensions, even if you choose to discard some."

12 "MOM," said Natalie the following Tuesday evening, when she had come home exhausted from work and was resting in the kitchen with her shoes off, "why didn't you ever tell me that Tallie had been married before?"

Her mother was stirring spaghetti sauce. She put the lid back on the heavy cast-iron pot, and turned to Natalie with a puzzled, surprised look.

"Nat, you're not going to believe this. In fact, if I were you, I *know* I wouldn't believe it. But I *forgot.*"

"You're right. I don't believe it."

"No, really. Of course, Stefan Chandler was my father. An incredible man. I so wish that you girls could have known him. And Tallie — my mother — *did* tell me that she'd been married before. I don't think she ever told me any of the details. It wasn't important. Tallie and Stefan were such a . . . well, how can I describe it? . . . theirs was such a good marriage. It was as if they must always have been together. They *adored* each other. They adored me, too, when I came along, and they made me part of it, of whatever they had."

"And you really didn't remember about her first husband?"

"No. Not until you mentioned it. But now I remember that she showed me a clipping once, his obituary — "

"It was twelve inches long, she said."

"Leave it to Tallie to make an obituary sound mildly obscene!" Kay Armstrong sat down at the kitchen table and smiled. "What else did she tell you?"

Natalie grinned. "That she was a terrible mother, and

you used to curl up in the corners of strange places and sleep because she forgot to put you to bed."

Her mother laughed affectionately. "Yes, I remember. She and Stefan used to take me everywhere. There were always loads of people — isn't it funny, how she's preferred solitude, since he's been dead? — and they would talk, and sing, and dance, and argue. After a while I would find myself a comfortable little spot somewhere and curl up, just the way she said.

"She's teasing, though, when she says she was a terrible mother. She was the best kind of mother. Did she tell you, though, that it hurt her dreadfully when I decided to marry?"

"It *did*? No, she didn't tell me that. Didn't she like Dad?"

"She does now. But then — well, I guess it was because he was so unlike Stefan. And Stefan had died only the year before. I think she hoped I would perpetuate that kind of wonderful crazy happiness by marrying someone exactly like him, so there would be three of us again."

"Was it hard for you, to disappoint her?"

Her mother thought. "No, strangely, it wasn't. Because I was all grown up then, and I knew what *she* wanted wasn't the same as what *I* wanted. I told her that. We were always very honest with each other. She understood. After a while, it was all right. She didn't tell you any of that?"

"Actually," said Natalie, "I guess she did. It was part of what she was saying."

13

TALLIE HAD SAID to wait until she had time, and solitude. They were both hard to come by. Her job took long hours of the day, frequently running over through dinnertime if there were patients still in the office; when she went home in the evenings, she went home still saturated with the burdens of other people's pain and with the stimulation of watching her father go about the intellectual and intuitive process of healing.

Most evenings, she saw Paul. He was working at a construction job, earning money that would help him through Yale. At night he would stop by, exhausted, and they sat on her porch, sipped iced tea, and talked. Sometimes she felt, sadly, that they had already entered two different worlds. His was the world of sunburn and sweat, and of men. When she asked him what he had done that day, he told her of the men he worked with — people she didn't know. Their talk, on the job, was of TV shows and women, Paul said, amused. They had asked him to join a bowling team and to drive with them to Boston some weekend for a Red Sox game.

High school seemed in the distant past, through it was only three weeks before that they had stood in the gym at graduation and whispered familiar jokes to their classmates, about teachers and shared pranks. Paul felt it too, the quickness of the transition. Two of their classmates had already joined the Navy; one other was married. The local newspaper had carried a picture of her on Sunday, wearing a white veil and smiling shyly over a bouquet of carnations. Four weeks before the same girl had been called into the principal's office for a lecture when she had been caught smoking in the girls' bathroom. Now she would be settling down in an apartment full of furniture sold in matched sets at Sears, joining the other housewives in their morning trips to the supermarket, carefully sorting the coupons from last night's paper, and waiting idly at the Laundromat while the week's wash floated like a collage in the dryer.

Another boy, someone they knew only slightly, had been killed two days after graduation, when he drove his car into a tree at midnight after a party. The Class of '77, which had stood in a proud group arranged according to height and wearing rented maroon graduation gowns, was already history. "What happened to ———" people would ask before long, and the answers would come, in many cases, as surprises. The Class Clown would be working in his father's company, selling radial tires. The Class Flirts, photographed for the yearbook in a silly, amorous pose, had gone separate ways, the girl to beauticians' school in Portland, and the boy studying aeronautics in New Hampshire. The Class Intellectual, Gretchen, was working in a summer camp in Vermont; Natalie had had a brief letter from her, filled with funny remarks about the crafts — basket-making and what Gretchen called "wavery weaving" — that she taught to rich people's children, and the news that Solzhenitsyn, in exile from Russia, was living only twelve miles away. On her day off she had passed the long fence that surrounded his house, and wanted, she wrote whimsically, to call over it "I love you."

"Here we are," said Natalie, laughing to Paul, "the 'Best All-Around Girl' and the 'Most Likely to Succeed Boy,' and we're too lazy to do anything except push this swing back and forth with our feet."

"And hold hands," added Paul, squeezing her hand. "Nobody ever said I was most likely to succeed *immediately*. And you're definitely the best all-around hand-holder I know."

"Oh, well. We'll set the world on fire someday. Right now it's nice to be lazy."

"You want to go to the movies Friday night?"

Natalie shook her head. "I'm leaving Thursday, and going to Simmons' Mills."

Paul sighed. "I really think you're crazy, Nat. You're going to go up there and talk to that lawyer — what was his name?"

"Foster H. Goodwin."

"You're going to go talk Foster H. Goodwin into telling you who your parents are, and then what? You're going to go knock on their door. I can see it now. They'll be living very peacefully in a split-level house, with five kids and a dachshund and a couple of Snowmobiles. Up comes Natalie Armstrong, up the front walk. Knock knock knock. 'Hello,' you'll say. 'Remember me?' What happens then?"

Natalie made a face at him. "Paul, give me credit for a little good sense. I don't know exactly what I'll do, but I'm certainly not going to march up to their front door. Maybe I'll write them a letter."

"Which they won't answer."

"Of course they'll answer. Probably they'll be really nice people. We'll have dinner together, or something.

They'll tell me a little bit about what happened seventeen years ago. We'll talk. I'll get to find out what they're like. They'll see what I'm like. We'll become friends. It won't be a big embarrassing deal, or anything."

"Then you'll exchange Christmas cards for the next thirty years."

Natalie laughed. "I *told* you. We'll become *friends*. And we won't have to wonder anymore whatever became of each other."

"It hasn't occurred to you that maybe they've never wondered at all?"

"Impossible," said Natalie firmly.

"Bullshit," said Paul. "I hope you're right, Natalie, for your sake. But I think you're the 'Best All-Around Crazy Person.'"

He gave the swing a strong push, and they moved suddenly back and forth, the way they had as children, trying to scare themselves into thinking they might fall. She held tightly to his hand.

 LATER THAT EVENING, after Paul had gone, Natalie opened the small box that Tallie had given her.

If I were Nancy, she thought, peeling away the Scotch tape at the edges, I would have opened this up as soon as I got off the boat from Ox Island. Nancy is the one who leaps in the ocean all at once. And I'm the one who goes in inch by excruciating inch.

For me, she thought, the waiting and the wondering are sometimes the best part of things. Maybe that's why I've kind of cooled it with Paul, when some of my friends have become so heavily involved. I like having things to look forward to.

She removed the lid from the box, and saw the letters that were written in her own mother's handwriting. She smiled. The small, vertical strokes of Kay Armstrong's script hadn't changed, though these letters had been saved for years. There were only a few; Tallie had sorted them, she had told Natalie, and given her just the ones that would add the necessary dimension. Natalie envisioned her grandmother looking through the stack, reading through each letter quickly, with her head cocked sideways like a bird, and making the selection, in the same way that Natalie had watched her paint with bold, carefully considered definitive strokes.

The first letter was dated March, 1960.

Dearest Tallie;

Aren't you *ever* going to cut loose from Boston just for a weekend and come to see us in Maine? The house is so spacious, and we have reserved a room for you; I painted it white, and there are plants hanging in the windows and a wonderful patch-work quilt on the bed, in all the shades of blue and green that are your favorites.

Alden is well, and *busy*. There is such a need for him here.

And I have made friends. There is lots to do, for a small town, even for someone like me who won't join a bridge group or go to cocktail parties. There are good people in Branford.

Alden had me see a gynecologist in Portland, and the news was disappointing, I'm afraid. The same old tests that I had in Boston, and the same old results. The same "It is very unlikely, Mrs. Armstrong —" etc. The same "Have you considered adoption, Mrs. Armstrong?"

We *have* registered with an adoption agency, but they are just as dreary to listen to as the doctors. My lord, Tallie, the paper-pushing that goes on! They seem to forget sometimes that they're dealing with humans. And with *babies*. They call them "our placements." "'Our placements' have a very high percentage of success." Ho hum. I don't care about their placements and percentages; I just want a *baby*, for pete's sake. Alden is much more patient and understanding of all the bureaucratic nonsense, and he makes a good impression on them, I'm sure, but then they look at me and stroke their chins and I suspect that they are thinking "Hmmmm . . . would one of our placements work with this crazy woman who wears jeans to an interview?"

And of course they cringed . . . tastefully, of course . . . when they asked about my family background. Turns out my education was what they call "unconventional." Can't imagine why! I thought having tutors come and go in Greece, France, Mexico, and Spain was great! Especially when they *went*, and left the three of us together and we all used to agonize over those schoolbooks and sometimes give up altogether. Remember when Stefan held a ceremonial Book-Burning of Algebra I when none of us could understand the fifth chapter?

Oh well. I wouldn't trade that for anything, but it is, apparently, making a "placement" difficult. In the meantime, I have left a small bedroom completely empty, waiting. I haven't given up hope, not at all.

But I would so like a child. A daughter, I confess. I daydream about holding her and singing some of those songs that you used to sing to me when I was small. Off-key, I might add.

Do come to visit. We could drink tea and sit by the fireplace and talk.

Much love,
Kay

June 10, 1960

Dearest Tallie,

Isn't it wonderful that we are living here, right on the way to Ox Island, so that there was no way you could not visit en route?

I loved having you here; so did Alden. It will take me a week to catch up on the lost sleep, but I have needed someone . . . especially you . . . to sit up with and talk to.

No, there is no new news from my visit to the agency. We have been officially approved, whatever that means . . . I suspect, from the way the woman looks at me, that they have stamped HIGHLY SUSPECT on our papers, but they do say that we passed all the necessary procedures, inspections, whatever.

But that seems to mean nothing, because then they tell us about the WAITING LIST, in hushed voices. Seems there is a LONG WAITING LIST.

Maybe I will just turn the empty bedroom into something useful, like a sewing room, or a place to keep plants, and try to forget that I wanted to hang bright pictures on the walls, and look in at night to see a baby sleeping there.

Oh, dammit, Tallie. You know, I try to be cheerful about it, but I want a baby so badly. Remember, when I was married, I said we would have one right away, and then another every year until there was a houseful? And now we have a houseful of emptiness, and I am so *sad*. Alden is so good, and says "Wait, wait," very patiently, but how can you wait forever for something you want so much?

I'm sorry to whine. But you will understand.

Much love,
Kay

July 12, 1960

Dearest Tallie,

I don't know where to begin this letter. I have been sitting here in the kitchen drinking tea and smiling, all by myself. Pour yourself a cup of tea while you read this and then smile with me.

Alden has been told by a lawyer whom we know slightly that there is a possibility of our adopting a baby privately. Not just "a baby," but a real one that is already in the making, that already exists! It is to be born in the fall.

I haven't been able to sleep since we heard. Alden is as always much more circumspect. He is carefully considering all the pros and cons, as he puts it . . . but I am quite, quite sure that we have already made the decision. He wants it as much as I do, and from what he was told, it won't be a surreptitious thing. All quite legal; just that we don't have to go through the long waiting period that the agency has been promising us.

Do you remember what it felt like to be waiting for your child to be born? This is no different from what it would be if I were pregnant. I am so excited . . . so scared. I worry about whether the baby will be born safely, and be healthy. I lie awake at night and think of all the things that I have waited so long for . . . to hold my own child, to teach it things, even to knit little sweaters, even though you know how undomestic I am!

I say "it" because I dont want to tempt fate, I suppose, but I feel very certain that it will be a little girl. Alden as usual pretends not to allow himself to be caught up by whims and emotions; he quotes statistics to point out that it is just as likely, more so actually, that it will be a boy. Then, last night, while we were having dinner, he suddenly smiled and said, "Let's name her for Tallie."

Will you like being a grandmother? Oh, how I wish Stefan were alive to share this with us all!

Much love,
Kay

August 29, 1960

Dearest Tallie,

Thank you, thank you for the wonderful surprise. When the package came, I couldn't imagine what it was . . . knowing that there are no stores on the island . . . and knowing that you wouldn't leave the island to go shopping, not even for an impending grandchild!

And there was my own childhood, packed so neatly into the box! That book of fairy tales in French; I remember your reading it to me . . . where did we live then? I was so small; I can remember the fireplace, and that there were blue bowls on a table, and that you had gold earrings that I used to reach for when you held me on your lap, but I can't remember where it was.

And those funny pictures that Stefan used to draw for me. I had no idea you had kept them! I am having them framed to hang in the baby's room. Some of them are quite indecent by Branford, Maine, standards . . . a nude Red Riding Hood . . . imagine! I remember laughing and laughing at that. Good thing the agency lady is no longer stopping by to check out our standards!

What fun it will be to share all of those things with my own child. Oh, Tallie, it is so hard to wait. I am knitting the most *terrible* sweater; the sleeves are different lengths even though I have ripped one of them out twice and re-done it. But it gives me something to do while the time goes by.

Much love,
Kay

NATALIE CHANDLER ARMSTRONG BORN YESTERDAY HEALTHY AND STRONG STOP ALDEN AND I WILL BRING HER HOME IN FOUR DAYS STOP WE ARE SO HAPPY TALLIE STOP   KAY

September 20, 1960

Dearest Tallie,

There is so much to say that I don't know where to begin, and I think I shall save most of it for when you come. When you close the house at Ox Island the end of the month, do plan to spend several days here on your way to Boston, won't you?

She is so beautiful that when I saw her, I wept.

Her hair is very dark, her features small, and her eyelashes quite long. Right now . . . she is sleeping here in the kitchen beside me . . . she looks exactly like the sleeping princess in the picture on page 16 of the fairy tale book you gave me; do you remember that picture, where the princess is waiting for the prince to arrive and wake her with a kiss? There was a time when I scoffed at that and thought it terribly over-romantic. But now I look at this beautiful child, sleeping, and realize that a whole world can lie before someone, if love is there when one wakes.

She is not at all like either of us, Alden or me, and I am glad. She will be her own person. It will be such a joy to watch her becoming that.

Much love,
Kay

Natalie laid the letters aside and closed her eyes. She remembered the book of fairy tales, which her mother had read to her in French, so that the language was strange and musical, and the sense of the tales was there only in the pictures, enhanced by that mysterious sound of words she didn't understand. Somewhere, she supposed, the book was packed away again, and would be there for her and Nancy to have for their own children.

The drawings that Stefan, her grandfather, had made with pen and ink were still there on the wall of her room. What an irrepressible man Stefan must have been! He had sat, her mother had told her, evenings at their kitchen table and illustrated for her, with his pen, as he told her the familiar stories that all children hear. His marvelous, meticulous drawings made them seem newly invented. There was Red Riding Hood, the one her mother's letter had mentioned, walking through woods thick with trees almost tropical in their growth, laden with strange flowers, and lurking with snakes and strange beasts almost hidden in the intricate foliage created by his pen. Red Riding Hood was naked, innocent in a child's nakedness, and her cloak flowed around her as she walked barefoot on the patch of the forest and looked upward with wide and trusting eyes to the heavy growth that surrounded her. There was humor and warmth to the drawing; but the fear was there, too.

It *is* another dimension, Natalie realized, as she got ready for bed. I always knew how much my parents had wanted me; it was one of the things they told me so often, when I was little, as a way of explaining my adoption. It makes it different, though, reading the letters, and knowing for the first time my mother as a young girl, really.

It explains their hurt, in a way. It doesn't change things. But it makes me understand everything more. "She will be her own person," the last letter said, and — she looked at it again — "It will be such a joy to watch her becoming that."

Well, I will make the trip to Simmons' Mills, and it will be done. The whole summer will be left, so that their joy will still be there and they will have time to get over the small hurt.

She looked at Stefan's drawing again before she turned out the light. It was filled with hidden things. The wolf himself was in a corner of the picture, so carefully drawn that he was himself part of the forest. She always had to search for him, when she was a child; and then, when she had found him, felt sad that she couldn't whisper into the picture and warn the naked child who walked barefoot with her eyes so full of innocent pleasure.

| 15 | THE ROAD to Simmons' Mills, beyond Bangor, as she had guessed from the map, was narrow, winding, and increasingly deserted. By five |

o'clock on Thursday Natalie was deep in the rugged, mountainous, awesome terrain of central Maine. The few drivers who passed her coming in the opposite direction were almost all huge lumber company trucks, heavy and noisy on the small road, their flatbeds piled with chained loads of massive logs from the woods.

She had filled the car's gas tank in Bangor, and was grateful that she had had the sense to do it, because there were no gas stations on this deserted road. No farmhouses. No tourist gift shops such as the ones along the coast, selling their plastic lobsters and varnished seashells. No restaurants. Twice she passed, seemingly in the middle of nowhere, general stores that advertised, in signs glued to their unpainted wooden walls, hunting and fishing licenses as well as Pepsi, beer, and pizza. She didn't stop, anxious to reach Simmons' Mills and find a place to stay before dark; the seedy stores disappeared into her rearview mirror and the woods closed around the road again.

To the west, she could see the sun hanging lower in the sky over the mountains: an incredible view from the top of each hill, as the road lifted itself now and then above the level of thick forest and held her there for a moment at a brief crest. She could see lakes, brilliant as broken glass in the reflected light of the low sun, to her left in the distance; and again and again she saw the river with its Indian name, Penobscot, surging heavily in its endless trip south to meet the ocean. Sometimes, she knew, the logs were sent south on the river in great log drives; she noticed, along its banks, occasional logs caught and wedged by rocks, held firmly there, perhaps forever, and causing the swift water to part and move around them in foamy interrupted patterns.

The woods, she knew, were filled with wild creatures: deer, moose, and bear, and the smaller animals that rustled the undergrowth and moved in and out of their deeply hidden burrows in search of food. She had never been, before, to the great central uninhabited part of Maine. It seemed a trip into a primeval time.

When from the top of a hill, suddenly, she could look down and see the town of Simmons' Mills spread like a small blemish beside the gray river and the vast deep green of woods, she pulled the car to the side of the road and stopped.

The forest parted only slightly for the town, as the river had reluctantly parted to surge around the caught logs. A huge paper mill stood by the river, its tall stacks spewing smoke that hung above them in flattened clouds and then dispersed, its gray tinged pink by the sun that was setting now. Natalie glanced at her watch uneasily; it was almost seven. She had, she realized, made this journey without sufficient preparation for the simple practicalities. She had expected a town to have motels. She had never *been* in a town without motels; now, looking down at Simmons' Mills as she eased the car back onto the road and started down the hill, she realized that Simmons' Mills was not a place that tourists would come to. From the hill, she could see that the outskirts, the place where one ordinarily found motels and restaurants, consisted only of a few farmhouses on land carved from the woods, placed at random like ornaments dangling from a string — the road — that fell in curves as if it had been dropped in haste.

She passed the farms, poor ones, with boulders in their pastures, and barn roofs sagging from the great weight of snow in winter, and drove into Simmons' Mills. One main street. She smiled, remembering that she had wondered briefly why Foster H. Goodwin's letter to her parents had had no street address. Now she realized that it wouldn't be necessary in a town the size of Simmons' Mills. But the telegram had directed her parents to 43 Main Street; she was passing that now: a brick building, two stories, with a drugstore on the ground floor. Offices upstairs, she supposed. That's where I will find Foster Goodwin. That's where, she realized suddenly, my parents came to get me. What a strange feeling it must have been, for them, to come to the top of that hill, to look down at this town, and to think "Our daughter is there."

Finally she breathed deeply and smiled in relief. Around the corner from Main Street, beside a church, she saw a white frame house with a sign in front of it: GUESTS.

Well, thought Natalie, I will be a guest in my own home town. She pulled her car into the driveway, and went to the front door.

The woman who answered her ring was pleasant, with a pink, lined face, bifocal glasses, and some knitting in one hand. From another room, Natalie could hear a television set; a familiar voice was giving the evening news in solemn tones. So Simmons' Mills isn't the end of the earth after all; they still listen to the news of wars and crime and disasters, Natalie thought. I bet they haven't had a crime here in years. Who would bother?

"Are you all alone, dear?" The woman glanced over Natalie's shoulder, toward her car.

"Yes. I need a place to stay tonight. Maybe tomorrow night, too."

"Well, I can give you a nice room. You'll have to share

the bathroom, but I only have one other guest right now. He's permanent; he works at the mill."

"That's fine." Natalie smiled. She was tired and hungry. The thought of a warm bath was inviting.

"It will be seven dollars a night. But that includes breakfast, dear." The woman sounded apologetic.

"All right. That sounds perfect. My name is Natalie Armstrong."

"And I'm Mrs. Talbot. Anna Talbot. Please come in, Natalie."

"Well, I'll get my things from the car, Mrs. Talbot. And is there someplace in town where I could get some supper?"

Mrs. Talbot frowned. "Oh, goodness. This is Thursday. I'm afraid every place is closed by now. On weekends, you know, there are places that stay open in the evening, but Thursday — well, you run out and get your bag, Natalie, and I'll fix you a bowl of soup and a sandwich. Would that be all right? I'll just add a little to your bill."

Natalie smiled gratefully and went to her car for her small suitcase. Every town, she thought, should have an Anna Talbot, to make strangers feel at home.

I bet anything, she thought, as she took her things to the room that Anna Talbot pointed out, that she knows my parents. As she washed her hands, she looked in the mirror. Her face was tired; it had been a long drive. I wonder, she thought, who it is in this town who has dark hair and blue eyes, like mine.

She sat in the kitchen, ate homemade vegetable soup and

a thick chicken sandwich, and drank a glass of milk. Anna Talbot hovered politely, making sure she didn't need anything else, and then took her knitting to the small sitting room where the television set was still on. When she was finished eating, Natalie rinsed her dishes in the sink, and then went tentatively to the door of the sitting room.

"That was delicious, Mrs. Talbot. Thank you."

"You're welcome, dear. Just let me know if you need anything."

"Well, I wondered if you might let me look at your telephone book, Mrs. Talbot. I have to see someone in Simmons' Mills tomorrow."

Anna Talbot chuckled. "Natalie," she said, "I'll give you the phone book." She reached to a nearby table and handed Natalie the thin volume. "But you could just ask me. I know everyone in this town. I can tell you where they live, whether they're home, how their health is, and who they voted for, for president."

Natalie laughed. "I came to the right place, then. You can probably tell me if Foster Goodwin's office is still at 43 Main Street. And whether I might be able to see him without an appointment, tomorrow."

Anna Talbot looked at her knitting, startled, as if she had dropped a stitch. Then she looked carefully at Natalie through the top half of her bifocals. Across the small room, the television screen had made the transition from a cheerful weatherman to a commercial for some kind of laundry detergent. A man in a white uniform was solemnly advising a frustrated housewife about the grease stains on her husband's shirt.

"Foster Goodwin," said Anna Talbot, puzzled, "has been dead for ten years."

16

Damn, THOUGHT NATALIE, and she felt the beginnings of tears rising hot behind her eyes. I am so *stupid*. I came up here like an idiot, expecting that everything would fall into place. Find Foster Goodwin, I thought. He's the only one who knows everything. Just find him, and he'll tell you. I *forgot* that it was seventeen years ago.

No, I didn't forget. But I thought it didn't matter. And of course it does. Everything changes in seventeen years. Foster Goodwin is dead. Now what?

I am so *tired* that I can't even think. I have to go to bed. But first I have to figure out what I'm going to do tomorrow. Somewhere in this strange town with one main street I can find my whole past, if I just figure out where to look. The doctor. What was his name? *He* was the one who delivered me; he'll know. He'll remember.

If he's alive. Natalie sighed, and sank down into the chair just inside the door to the sitting room. Anna Talbot was watching her. She had begun again to knit, her fingers moving automatically, lifting the yarn behind the needle again and again. Under her hands a blue mitten was taking shape.

"You look very tired, dear."

"Yes," said Natalie, "I am. It was a long drive." (What

was his name? What was his name? The letters are up-stairs in my suitcase, and I'm too tired to move.)

"Rest for a minute, Natalie," said Anna Talbot. "I'll make tea, and we can talk. Look — " she held up the mitten. "For my latest grandchild. I haven't ever seen him, and he's almost two. But they live in Kentucky. It's such a long trip."

Natalie looked around the room, and saw the framed photographs of grandchildren — all ages, some infants, some in graduation gowns. School pictures, their colors too bright, their smiles too forced. Snapshots, blurred, of children holding up fish, of young girls posing in party dresses, boys beaming in front of new bicycles, new babies dangled in front of an amateur camera.

"You have a big family, don't you, Mrs. Talbot?"

"Sixteen grandchildren," the woman said proudly. "Five children. All of my children grew up here and graduated from Simmons' Mills High School. Two of them graduated from college. Of course, I don't see them often enough. They've all gone away. Very few people *stay* in Simmons' Mills — young people, that is. My own children have all gone away years ago. But they write."

"You must miss them," said Natalie politely.

Anna Talbot smiled. "It's lonely, sometimes. My hus-band has been dead five years, now."

It's lonely, sometimes. What a sad thing, Natalie thought, to be lonely. I've never really thought of it be-fore. Because Tallie is alone, and not lonely; Tallie loves the aloneness, though she misses Stefan still, even after all these years.

"Mrs. Talbot, I'd love some tea," said Natalie. "I just want to get something from my room."

She rose, went to the tidy bedroom at the top of the stairs, and took the letters from her suitcase. There it was. "The family was referred to me by Dr. Clarence Therrian," Foster Goodwin — the *late* Foster Goodwin (she winced) — had written.

Please, thought Natalie, coming down the stairs, let Clarence Therrian be alive. Because if he isn't, I don't know what to do next.

Anna Talbot poured tea from a graceful pot decorated with pink roses and thin gold lines. So different from Tallie's thick pottery that had in it memories of earth and strong hands. But this was more appropriate for Anna Talbot. Natalie thanked her and sipped her tea from a fragile cup.

"Mrs. Talbot," she said. "I came here because I need some information that Foster Goodwin had. The only other person who might be able to help me is a doctor named Clarence Therrian." *Please*, thought Natalie again. Please. When she was a child, her mother had called it a magic word.

"Poor Clarence," sighed Anna Talbot, taking up her knitting again, "poor, dear Clarence."

He's dead, too, thought Natalie, and her stomach wrapped itself around the warm tea in a tight and painful knot.

"I sent him a plant the other day," said Anna Talbot. "A cutting from that coleus in the kitchen. I potted it in a lovely little green pot that I'd been saving for something special. Poor Clarence. I hope he's able to enjoy it."

"What do you mean?"

"You don't know Clarence, dear?"

"No."

"A dear man. He was the only doctor in Simmons' Mills for years and years. He delivered all my children. He cared for my husband until he died. Now, of course, there are other doctors. In the past few years, young people seem to want to come to a place like this. So there are three young doctors in town now. All with beards." She grimaced. "Can you imagine, being examined by someone with a beard? Poor Clarence. He was always so meticulous about his appearance."

"What do you mean, was? He isn't dead, is he? You said you just sent him a plant."

"Oh, no. But he's very, very ill. Poor Clarence." She lowered her voice to a whisper, as if her news were scandalous. "He had a, you know, a growth."

Cancer, thought Natalie. How often she had heard the relatives of her father's patients refuse to say the word.

"Of course, he's much older than I am," Anna Talbot quickly pointed out, as if she were thereby eliminating the possibility of its happening to her. "You know" — and she was speaking in a semiwhisper again — "there was a *feeling*, in the town, after Clarence's wife died two years ago, that perhaps he and I — well." She took a tiny pair of scissors from her knitting basket, snipped off her yarn, and held up a finished mitten. "That was silly, of course. Clarence and I have been friends for years. He's a *dear* man. Perhaps I mentioned that already. But he's *much* older than I. I think he's at least eighty.

"It's dreadful that he's all alone now. They lost their only child very young, and then Mary passed away — such a crowd at her funeral, dear. They were such loved people in this town. But he has no family left, and that's why I took it upon myself to send the plant. I wouldn't want you to think it was anything more than that, dear." Anna Talbot looked up shyly, and she was blushing. Natalie felt a surge of affection and pity for the woman.

"Where is he, Mrs. Talbot?"

"Oh, he's in the hospital, dear. The Simmons' Mills Community Hospital, just beyond the mill, on the river road."

"Do you think I could see him?"

Mrs. Talbot's face wrinkled into a frown. "I couldn't say. I understand he's very bad now. Is it terribly important?"

Natalie nodded. "Yes," she said, "it really is."

"Let me think," said Mrs. Talbot. "I'll call Winnie Bailey if you like. She's one of the nurses at the hospital. She'd know."

"Oh, would you? Thank you."

Anna Talbot picked up the phone on the table by her chair and dialed. Natalie poured more tea into both their cups.

"Winnie, dear? It's Anna Talbot. I hope I haven't taken you away from one of your programs.

"Well, I'll just be a minute. I wanted to ask how Clarence is.

"Yes, I know, isn't it sad? Of course he's older than we are, Winnie.

"Do you happen to know if he received the plant I sent

over on Tuesday? No, well, there's no reason he would mention it, of course. I'm sure he has scads of flowers. It *is* in an especially nice green pot, though, if you should happen to notice.

"Well, I have a guest here, Winnie, who would like to see him.

"I'm not sure. No, she isn't related, I don't think. But she would just like to talk to him for a *minute*."

Anna Talbot covered the receiver with one hand and whispered to Natalie. "It wouldn't take long, would it, dear?" Natalie shook her head no.

"All right, Winnie, I'll tell her that. Thank you. You go back to your television now, dear. Goodbye."

Anna Talbot was quiet for a minute, and then she sighed. "It's as I thought. He's doing very poorly. Poor Clarence."

"But I can see him for a minute?" asked Natalie.

"You're to go over around eleven in the morning, dear. Ask for Winnie Bailey, and she'll take you in."

Natalie finished her tea and suddenly she was overwhelmingly exhausted. She stood up. "Mrs. Talbot, I can't thank you enough. You've been such a help to me. Now I have to get some sleep."

"Of course, dear. If you want an extra blanket, they're in the chest in your room. And I wonder, dear, if you would do one small favor for me?"

"Of course."

"When you see Clarence, would you point out to him the coleus in the green pot? And tell him that it's from Anna Talbot?"

17 FRIDAY WAS CLEAR and cloudless over Simmons' Mills, with a sky so blue it could have been colored in by a child who had saved his very best crayon for the effect. Natalie left her car at Mrs. Talbot's and walked to the hospital.

The town, brightened by the sun in morning, seemed less gray than it had the night before. The buildings on the main street were old ones, but the wood was painted, the bricks were clean, and there were people entering and leaving the few stores, the bank, the library, and the post office. At night, it had seemed a movie-set town, left behind after the actors had gone away; in the daytime, Natalie realized, walking toward the mill that dominated the north edge of the town with its silhouette, it was simply an ordinary small town, one in which lives were being lived, it appeared, with contentment and a kind of quiet charm.

My mother walked here, she thought, waiting for me to be born.

The hospital was new: modern, stark, and efficient, with the vaguely antiseptic smell that bright-figured draperies and Matisse prints never seem to dispel in hospitals. Entering by the front door, Natalie saw in the lobby a young doctor, bearded, and smiled. *Imagine* being examined by a man with a beard, Mrs. Talbot had said. He smiled at her with interest in return, but she turned away, to the woman behind the information desk.

"I'm looking for someone named Winnie Bailey," she said. "A nurse."

The woman nodded. "Second floor," she said, pointing to a flight of stairs. "Up there and to your left."

Winnie Bailey was behind the nursing station on the second floor, and she looked up and nodded when Natalie appeared. "You're the one Anna called about," she said.

"Yes. My name is Natalie Armstrong."

"You know, Dr. Therrian is very ill," the woman said. Natalie nodded.

"He hasn't been allowed visitors. But he's been feeling a little better for the past two days, and I've checked with his doctors. It's all right if you see him, but only briefly. Of course you won't be upsetting him, will you? You haven't brought bad news?"

"Oh, I don't think so," said Natalie. "I just need a little information that I think he has, about someone who was a patient of his a long time ago."

Winnie Bailey wrinkled her forehead. "Goodness. That might be a problem. He's feeling pretty well this morning, but of course he's on a lot of medication, and his mind *does* wander. You may find that he won't be able to understand what it is you want."

Oh, he has to, thought Natalie. He *must*. "I'll just have to try," she said. "It's so important to me."

"Would you like me to go in with you?"

"I don't think so," said Natalie. "It will be all right."

"Well then, it's room 234, just down the hall there. I wouldn't stay more than fifteen minutes." Winnie Bailey smiled and picked up some folders and her pen.

The door to room 234 was partially open, and hung with signs. NO VISITORS. NO SMOKING. Natalie pushed it gently with her hand and looked inside to where on old man lay alone. His eyes were closed, his face pale against the pillow, and a bottle of glucose dangled from its rack beside his bed, attached to his left arm by the narrow plastic tube that dripped the solution in measured drops into his vein. There were vases of flowers on the wide windowsill, and among them was the green pot of coleus. Natalie smiled. She went closer to the bed.

"Dr. Therrian?" she said softly.

He turned his head and blinked his eyes. He stared at her for a moment, and then looked around the room as if he had lost his bearings, as if he were reassessing where he was.

"I'm sorry to wake you," Natalie said.

The old man turned to her again, looked at her carefully, looked at her hair, at her face, moved his eyes along her blue sweater, back to her face again. Then he reached out his hand, and took hers, and smiled.

"Julie?" he said.

THIS IS SO HARD, thought Natalie. How can I
18 torment this old, tired, sick man with my questions? He can't even understand what's going on. His mind is wandering. He thinks I'm someone else. He's probably in pain. I should just leave him alone.

But I have come all this way. And he's the only one who can help me.

She said gently, "Dr. Therrian. My name is Natalie."

"Julie?" he said again.

"No," she answered. "I'm not Julie. My name is Natalie. I've come a long way to see you. Can you hear me?"

He nodded.

"I can't stay long because the nurse said that you need to rest. So I'll try to explain this quickly."

He was watching her intently, and his hand was still in hers. It was cold, and she held it tightly to warm it.

"You delivered me, Dr. Therrian. Seventeen years ago."

He smiled. "Many," he said.

"Yes, you delivered many babies. Is that what you mean?"

He nodded.

"I was special, in a way, though, because for some reason my mother couldn't keep me." It was hard for her to say it.

He closed his eyes and nodded his head again.

"You remember her, don't you, Dr. Therrian?"

"Blue eyes," the old man said.

Natalie bit her lip. "Yes. They said she had blue eyes and dark hair. Dr. Therrian, I want very much to find her now."

He was watching her again, and he didn't say anything.

"Would you tell me her name? Do you remember her name?"

He gripped her hand suddenly, and she realized from his face, as it drew tight and his eyes closed, that a spasm of pain had overwhelmed him. She waited, and felt pain herself, for this man who was so alone and so close to death.

Finally he relaxed. "Dr. Therrian," Natalie said, "I'm

so sorry that I have to bother you like this. But there is no one else who knows; do you understand?"

He nodded, and said softly, "You look like her. I thought you were Julie."

The short sentences had tired him, she could tell. He was breathing deeply, and he took his hand away from hers, as if he wanted to go to sleep. Natalie felt agony for him, and desperation for herself. She tried again.

"Please don't talk. I'll just ask you questions, and you can nod your head yes or no. Maybe that will be easier."

He sighed and nodded.

"You do remember my mother," Natalie began.

He nodded.

"She came to you because she was going to have a baby. She had blue eyes. I look like her; that's why you called me Julie when I came in?"

He nodded.

There is so much, Natalie thought, that I am not going to be able to ask him. What kind of woman was she? Did she work? Did she have other children? He doesn't have the strength to answer questions like that. I must find out from him who she *is*; then I can ask *her* those things.

"You helped to arrange my adoption, with Foster Goodwin. Do you remember?"

He nodded.

"What about my *father*? Did you know him, too? Did he come with her to your office?"

The old man stared at her. His head didn't move.

"Was it that the woman — Julie — wasn't married, Dr. Therrian? Is that why she had to give me away?"

He nodded.

"I have to ask you to tell me one more thing, Dr. Therrian, so that I can find her. Can you tell me Julie's last name?"

It was an effort, she could tell, for him to speak. He was exhausted. But he said, "Jeffries. Julie Jeffries."

So there it was. Her mother's name. I have come such a long way, thought Natalie, as she had thought before, and it was for those two words.

"Is she here, Dr. Therrian? In Simmons' Mills?"

He shook his head. And she felt it all slipping away again, the search that she thought would be a simple one.

"Do you know where she is?"

He shook his head no.

"Dr. Therrian," Natalie said, knowing she must leave, that she had already exhausted him, and had stayed too long, "I'm just going to repeat it, to make sure that I have it right. Then I'll go, and you can sleep.

"She came to you; she wasn't married; she was going to have a child. You delivered me, and Foster Goodwin made the arrangements for the adoption. Afterward she went away; she isn't here in Simmons' Mills anymore. But the name of the woman who is my mother was Julie Jeffries."

He had been watching as she spoke and nodding. Suddenly his head turned, and he was shaking his head in disagreement. Some part of it was wrong.

Winnie Bailey had appeared in the doorway and was motioning Natalie to leave.

"What's wrong, Dr. Therrian?" she asked. "What part of it did I get wrong?" She leaned close to him, and he spoke softly to her, but with firmness.

"Julie Jeffries was not a woman," he said. "She was a child. She was fifteen years old."

19

So WHAT'S the big deal? Natalie asked herself as she walked back along the main street of Simmons' Mills. Paul told you you might find out something you didn't want to know. It could have been worse. Fifteen-year-old girls get pregnant all the time.

I just have to revise my vision of my mother, that's all. Natalie kicked a pebble across the sidewalk, like a child, and answered herself.

Don't kid yourself. You're really bugged by what he told you. You wanted your mother to be someone noble, not a dumb scared kid.

I don't know what I *wanted*. It's just that it took me by surprise. I don't know what I think about it.

You're *mad*. That's what you think. You're mad at your own mother, seventeen years ago, and that's about the stupidest reaction you could have.

I'm not mad. I'm thinking.

And you're disappointed in her.

No, I'm not. I'm not even thinking about her. I'm thinking about that poor old man, all alone, dying.

Julie Jeffries must have felt all alone, too.

Big deal. She should have thought of *that* before she started screwing around.

Ha! You *are* mad.

Well, why shouldn't I be? What a dumb thing for a kid to do. She really loused up her life. Mine too.

You're the one that loused up your life. By coming here. By nosing around, disturbing people, just to find out things that would break your heart.

Knock it off. My heart's not broken. No way.

Then why are you crying?

I'm not.

And Natalie wiped the tears from her face with the back of her hand, took a deep breath, and walked through Simmons' Mills, watching the kids ride their bikes down the main street, calling to each other through the sun-bright air. As Julie Jeffries had.

20 "MRS. TALBOT, I'm going to stay one more night if that's okay."

"Certainly, dear. Did Clarence give you the information you needed?"

"Yes, sort of. He's a nice man. Your plant is on his windowsill."

"Oh, lovely. You did mention it to him, didn't you, that it was I who sent it? Sometimes those nurses just throw away the cards, I think."

"Yes," Natalie lied. "He was very pleased."

Anna Talbot sighed with pleasure, and leaned forward to adjust the television.

"I'm going out for some lunch now, and then to the library. I'll be back later."

"The library? I believe Winnie Bailey's niece is the librarian now. Wonderful girl. Too bad she married that fellow from Machias; *anyone* in Simmons' Mills could have told her it wouldn't work out, but you know how some young girls are when they think they're in love. Well, at least she has a beautiful set of twins. They won the Baby Contest at the Fourth of July celebration two summers ago and their picture was in the Bangor paper. Are you doing some kind of historical research at the library, dear?"

Natalie grinned. "Yes," she said. "I guess you could call it that."

Such a small, small town, Natalie mused as she left the house. No secrets in Simmons' Mills. Anna Talbot could tell me about my mother. I'd only need to ask her what girl in this town gave birth to an illegitimate baby in the fall seventeen years ago. Her knitting would fall into her lap, dropping stitches that would leave flaws in her grandchild's mittens; her eyes would open wide behind her glasses; she'd look at me, with my face that looks like Julie's face, and she'd remember. She'd tell me everything.

She'd also tell everyone else in Simmons' Mills. The phone company would have an overload for two days.

And I can't do that to Julie Jeffries. It was her secret. I'll make it mine, but we'll leave it that way.

The Simmons' Mills Library (donated, according to the bronze plaque, in memory of those sons of Simmons' Mills who lost their lives during World War I) was small, squat, and somber. In Branford, the library had been renamed the Media Center, and redecorated in bright colors, with squishy plastic chairs; rising from them, barelegged, in summer, was like removing a Band-Aid. In Simmons' Mills, a visiting reader still sat upright and rigid, under dim light, and in silence.

Not for long, though, thought Natalie, looking at the young, freckled librarian seated behind the desk. The rectangular holder at the edge of the desk held a small plastic sign that said Ms. Farley. The picture frame in the corner held a photograph of two identical babies in striped sunsuits. Ms. Farley was leafing through the pages of the latest *Cosmopolitan*; she put it down, open to a quiz for testing one's sex appeal, looked at Natalie, and smiled. "Hi there," she said.

Ms. Farley, thought Natalie, you'll have them talking out loud in the Simmons' Mills Library for the first time. Good for you.

"Hi. I'd like to see some old newspapers from Simmons' Mills."

Ms. Farley raised her eyebrows. "Hope you're not looking for *news*. The last exciting thing that happened around here was when the FBI machine-gunned those gangsters down in Bangor. And that was 1937."

Natalie laughed. "No, I just want to check on some people who used to live here. I figured there might be something in the paper — local social notes, that sort of thing."

"Well, we have the papers themselves back to 1950. Before that, they're on microfilm."

Natalie calculated quickly. "1959, 1960, around there, is what I want."

"No problem. Unless you're allergic to dust. They're in the back room." Ms. Farley pointed toward a door behind her desk. "Can you find them yourself? I'd help you, but I'm not supposed to leave the main area" — she grimaced — "unguarded." Natalie and the librarian looked toward the one inhabited table, where three small children were turning the pages in picture books, forming the words of the brief texts with their mouths solemnly.

"It's okay," Natalie said. "I'll poke around by myself."

"Well." Ms. Farley grinned. "Yell if you need help. But yell quietly." She nodded toward the small sign tacked to the wall: "Please remember that a library is a place for learning. Respect the needs of others by your silence." Ms. Farley winked.

"Thank you," whispered Natalie, chuckling, and opened the door behind the librarian's desk.

The back room was walled with shelves. She found the local newspaper, stacked by years, removed the stacks marked 1959 and 1960, and blew the dust from the top of each pile. Then she set them on the table that was in the center of the small room. She was not at all sure, she realized, what she was looking for. Certainly there would not be a birth announcement.

Still, it was a very small town. Just how small was even more evident as she turned the first few pages idly and read at a glance the notices of 4-H meetings, of Boy Scout awards, and of church suppers.

In December of 1959, the Simmons' Mills Baptist Church had postponed its Christmas pageant because of a severe snowstorm.

In December of 1959, Natalie realized, Julie Jeffries became pregnant. Tough to do, she thought cynically, in a town this size, knee-deep in snow. She must have found a warm place. They. They must have found a warm place.

The pageant was held a week later: a great success; rave reviews. A blurred photograph showed the cast. The Virgin was a blonde, with a crooked cardboard halo, and an embarrassed smile; her name was Jackie McNabb.

She was probably a friend of Julie's, thought Natalie, looking thoughtfully at the badly focused photograph of the pretty girl selected as 1959's Baptist Virgin. Julie must have looked at this picture. She must have been having some heavy thoughts, that Christmas, about virginity in general.

Natalie turned the pages. The high school glee club gave a Christmas concert, but the names of the singers were not listed. The Simmons' Mills Library had held a Christmas party for children, with a Santa Claus who distributed the edible decorations from the tree. Mrs. Edith Morrow was visiting her sister in Portland for the holidays. Edgar Moreau had injured himself when he fell against his chain saw; forty stitches were required, but he was doing well at the local hospital. Vandals had thrown beer cans in the cemetery. Patrolman Michael Moreau (Edgar's son? It didn't say) had been promoted to sergeant on the Simmons' Mills three-man police force and would be driving the new cruiser. School would reopen on the 3rd of January if the leaks in the roof were repaired by then; the repair work was being undertaken by W. D. Corning and Sons.

On January 2nd, the first baby of the New Year was born at Simmons' Mills Community Hospital, and was photographed asleep, wearing a banner that said 1960. It was a boy, named Dennis Paul Moreau, the first child of Michael and Jeannine Moreau (how about that, thought Natalie; Mike got a promotion and a son the same week. Congratulations), and was delivered at 9:20 A.M. (you missed your income tax deduction, though, Mike; hope the raise made up for it) by Dr. Clarence Therrian.

She thought of the old man and the way he had looked at her. The way he said, "Julie?" Did he remember all of his patients that way?

On January 6th, Mr. and Mrs. Clement Jeffries had held an Open House for the executives of the P. R. Simmons Paper Company, at their home on Falls Road.

She sat down. Those *had* to be Julie's parents. Those were — *are* — my grandparents. Mr. and Mrs. Clement Jeffries.

Natalie wrote down their names and Falls Road. Julie has gone away, Dr. Therrian said; but her parents may still be there. They can tell me where she is. If they will.

I'll make up a story about why I want to find her. She's an old friend of my mother, I'll tell them.

I can't. They'll recognize me. Dr. Therrian recognized me, and called me Julie.

I'll talk to them on the phone, then.

And everything seemed simple again.

Natalie leafed hastily through other papers. On January 15, 1960, Simmons' Mills High School listed its honor roll.

Julie Jeffries, a sophomore, had all As and Bs. Only one sophomore, Margo McLellan, had all As. Natalie felt a twinge of dislike for Margo McLellan.

She put the newspapers back on their shelf, opened the door, and found Ms. Farley reading a story to the three small children, one of them in her lap, stroking the librarians's hair gently as he listened.

Natalie waited until the brief story was finished. "Ms. Farley," she asked, "could I see the phone book?"

The librarian sighed, lifted the little boy down from her lap, and came over to the desk. "Sure," she said, handing Natalie the small telephone directory, "but I'm really sorry. I can't let you use the phone. It's an idiotic rule. The theory is that if we let *one* person use the phone, *everyone* will want to use the phone. I've never figured out what disaster will take place if everyone uses the phone.

"Boy," she confided suddenly, "wait till next year. Next year when Mrs. Rhea retires, I'm taking over as head librarian. You come back next year, you can use the phone, whistle, hum, without a signed permission slip from your mother —"

"It's okay." Natalie laughed. "I don't want to use the phone, anyway. I just want to look something up."

Clement Jeffries was not listed.

Now what, thought Natalie. For a minute there I thought I was really a hot-shot detective. Boy, if they'd put me on the Watergate assignment, Nixon would still be in office.

"Do you by any chance," she asked, returning the telephone book, "have old yearbooks from Simmons' Mills High School?"

Ms. Farley groaned. "You've really made my day," she said. "Yes, we have the yearbooks. But now I have to read you *this*." She took a paper from the desk drawer, glanced at it, and recited, "'In the past, certain people have abused their library privileges by defacing the high school yearbooks that are kept here. It should be clearly understood that anyone who marks these books in any way, particularly with obscene drawings or remarks, will be held liable for the replacement costs and will have their library privileges suspended for one year.'"

Natalie crossed her heart earnestly. "I promise I will not deface the yearbooks," she said. "Cross my heart and hope to die."

"You won't draw big breasts with a ball-point pen on the gym teacher?" asked Ms. Farley, grinning.

"I will not draw big breasts with a ball-point pen on the gym teacher," promised Natalie, giggling. "Honest."

"Okay, then. What year?"

"1960."

"Darn," said Ms. Farley. "If you'd asked for 1970, you could have seen me as homecoming queen, freckles and all." She laughed and found the 1960 book in a locked closet lined with shelves.

The 1960 Simmons' Mills yearbook was dark green and was called "The Oracle." The school colors were green and gold, and the yearbook was dedicated to Herman Wright, who was retiring after thirty years of teaching shop.

Julie Jeffries looked exactly like Natalie. She had expected that, but the surprise of seeing it was so great that her knees shook, and she had to sit down.

"You okay?" asked Ms. Farley, watching her.

"Yes," said Natalie slowly. "I'm okay. Thank you for everything."

	NATALIE SPRAWLED crosslegged on the bed in
21	her room at Mrs. Talbot's, looked through her
	notes, and summarized what she had learned

about her mother. She had spent almost two hours seated
at the library table, reading the yearbook from cover to
cover.

Julie Jeffries was not in the 1961 yearbook; she had not
returned to Simmons' Mills High School for her junior
year. She was also not there as a freshman.

Someone named Julie Jeffries, who had long dark hair
and light blue eyes, had spent one school year in Simmons'
Mills, Maine. She had been there from the beginning of
her sophomore year, apparently, because she was a cheerleader. Cheerleading tryouts were always held at the very
beginning of a school year. Julie had been pictured smiling
and posing with five other girls, wearing short plaid skirts
and dark sweaters with a large SM on them. Saddle shoes
and knee socks. Her dark hair long and straight, with
bangs. Lipstick: this was 1959.

She was probably the daughter of Mr. and Mrs. Clement
Jeffries, who had lived on Falls Road. They were listed
in the 1959 and 1960 telephone directories; there were no
other Jeffries in Simmons' Mills. Clement Jeffries was
very probably an executive of the P. R. Simmons Paper
Company, the same mill that was on this sunny Friday
sending heavy yellow fumes over the town.

Julie had been on the honor roll. She was also on the
girls' field hockey team that fall and a member of the
French Club.

She attended the Christmas formal. Natalie found her
in the crowd in a yearbook picture, wearing a floor-length

net-skirted gown, ruffled around the shoulders, with a corsage, smiling, holding the hand of a tall, dark-haired boy whose face was turned away and blurred. Damn, Natalie had thought, studying the picture. That is *probably* my father, and he didn't have enough sense to hold still when the picture was taken.

She had been in the school Dramatic Club, as well, and in November had appeared as Cleopatra in Shaw's *Caesar and Cleopatra*. Natalie blinked in astonishment, looking for a long time at the yearbook photograph of Julie in the role. She was stunning. She was slender, sophisticated for her age (maybe only fourteen then, in November?), heavily made up for the role, with dark shiny color above her eyes, and her hair heavy, her mouth petulant and seductive, as Shaw had written the young Cleopatra to be.

In other pictures, she was simply a very young, very beautiful high school girl, usually laughing.

What else do I know? In December she became pregnant (by whom? Probably the boy who took her to the dance on the 23rd; who is he? No way to know). She would have realized that by what? February, probably; or at least she would have been scared stiff by February; by March, for sure. It may not have shown, three months along. But at some point — say March — she went to Dr. Therrian. Did her parents know?

Would she have finished the school year? Can't tell; the yearbook pictures are all taken before Christmas. The school year ended here in late May; she would have been five months pregnant then. Funny thing; that was the year (she had realized, from the yearbook) that those awful "sack" dresses were in style. Julie could have pulled it off, could have finished her sophomore year without anyone knowing she was pregnant.

Then what? She had stayed in Simmons' Mills. Dr. Therrian had delivered the baby (my Lord: me!) in September. It must have been a horrible summer for her. This isn't the sort of town where one goes unnoticed.

And then she, and her parents (and other kids? No other Jeffries in the high school, at least), had moved away.

Where? And where is she now?

Natalie thrust the notes into her suitcase and went out to her car. Falls Road wouldn't be hard to find, she thought. There are so few streets in this town.

It wasn't. It was, in fact, very close to the hospital, just beyond the huge brick smoke-spewing mill. Falls Road turned off River Road in a curve, crossed the Penobscot on a narrow bridge, and moved in a gradual bend up the hills until it overlooked the town of Simmons' Mills. There were very few houses on Falls Road; Natalie counted seven at wide intervals before the road ended in a circular turn at the top of the wooded hill.

This is where the rich guys live, she thought. I have to add that, then, to my notes. Julie Jeffries was a rich kid. And there weren't very many of them in Simmons' Mills. I wonder if she was a snob; I wonder if she had a lot of friends. She had one friend who made her pregnant. Some friend.

Natalie slowed the car when she saw a gray-haired woman at the end of a long driveway, removing the mail from a box marked "Petrie" in carefully painted Gothic script.

"Excuse me," she said, stopping. The woman looked up, startled, and then smiled when she realized it was a young girl. Not a crank; not a vandal; not a potential mugger.

"Yes?"

"I'm, ah, looking," Natalie said, frantically trying to remember the story she had prepared and hadn't needed to use yet, "for someone who knows something about someone who used to live here."

"Goodness. Could you say that again?"

Not for a million dollars, thought Natalie. It sounded so stupid. "I'm sorry." She laughed. "My cousin used to live in Simmons' Mills a long time ago. I thought, since I was here, I'd drive past her old house so I could tell her I'd seen it. But I've forgotten which one she said it was."

"What is her name, dear?"

"Jeffries. It was Mr. and Mrs. Clement Jeffries who owned the house."

The woman laughed. "Well, they didn't *own* the house, dear. These houses are all owned by the mill. But yes, I know which one it was, because it's the one I live in now. The Jeffries were here just before we came. I believe they were here only a short time?"

Natalie nodded. "Just a year. But, ah, my cousin has very fond memories of the house."

"Well —" The woman hesitated. "I could show you the inside if you'd like, but I'm expecting guests for the weekend, and I'm afraid —"

"No," said Natalie. "That's all right. But could I just drive up the driveway and look at the outside?"

"Certainly," said the woman. "In fact, you can give me a lift back to the house. It's not far, but it's uphill."

She got into the car, and Natalie drove slowly up the winding narrow driveway. The house was barely visible from the road.

"It's very large," the woman said. "A terrible house to take care of. They built them so big back then. These houses were all built, oh, I think around the 1880s, when people had servants. See?"

The driveway widened into a circular area in front of the house, and Natalie stopped the car and looked up with awe. There were actually turrets at the corners. The front door was heavy oak, carved in an intricate design.

"'Last night I dreamt I was at Manderley again,'" Natalie quoted, smiling.

The woman laughed. "Yes. It's like a Gothic novel, isn't it? You should have to vacuum it, though. My grandchildren adore it — there are back stairs, and dark hallways, and cubbyholes, and the towers, of course. It's fun, for them. But try keeping it clean." She sighed, and got out of the car. "Well, tell your cousin — what was her name?"

"Jeffries. Julie Jeffries. She's older than I am, of course. She was a kid when she lived here."

"Tell her you saw it, and it's still standing, but there is dust in every corner. I hope her mother had more energy than I do."

Natalie smiled. "Yes, I'll tell her."

"Will you be seeing her soon? I can't remember where they moved to."

Natalie smiled again and waved. "Thank you for letting me see it. She'll be pleased. Yes, I'll be seeing her later this summer. Bye."

She drove down the curving driveway again, and in the rearview mirror saw the turrets disappear behind the thick pine trees. Yes, I *will* be seeing her later this summer. If I can find her.

22

"NATALIE, you're so *dumb*."

Natalie leaned over and punched Paul affectionately on the arm. He had become very tanned, from work; she felt pale and pasty white, herself. Working all day in an office didn't lend itself to beach trips or tennis, and it had rained the past two weekends.

"You're getting muscles you never had before," she told him. "Big bronze god. Why am I dumb?"

He rolled over and lay on his back in the grass. They were in Natalie's yard, loafing. Thinking up things to do. Saying "Why don't we —" to each other. Then not doing anything. Saturday afternoon laziness. It was good, just being with Paul. She hadn't seen him for a while.

"Because," he said. "Listen, when did I talk to you last?"

"A week ago. You rat. What have you been doing?"

"Messing around with the guys." He grinned. She punched him again.

"No, listen, really," Paul said, more seriously. "I really

have been thinking about what you told me. About the whole Nancy Drew bit."

"Mmmmmm?"

"Why haven't you done anything more since you came back from that town — what's it called?"

"Simmons' Mills. Because I haven't figured out what to do next."

"Liar. Because you're scared."

She thought about what he had said. "Maybe," she admitted finally. "It's weird, Paul. I find out something, and then — well, it's almost as if that's *enough*. I start thinking that maybe I don't *want* to find out the rest. And when it gets tough, knowing where to look next, I guess I kind of use that as an excuse."

"Are you ready to quit, then? Give it up?"

She stared at the sky. A few clouds moved slowly, their undersurfaces touched with gray, a hint of rain, but no real threat to the day; they disappeared behind the thick leaves of the maple tree and the sun still flickered in patterns across the grass and their bare feet.

"No." She sighed. "I don't want to give it up."

"Well, then. I have it all figured out. What you should have done."

"Thanks a lot," Natalie said sarcastically. "I thought I was a pretty good detective."

"Yeah? You didn't find out much, did you?"

"Did too. I found out who my mother is, for pete's sake. I just didn't find out *where* she is."

"Okay, listen. You should have gone to the local Episcopal church. People like that are always Episcopalians."

"What do you mean, people like that? *I'm* Episcopalian."

"Big deal. That's just what I meant. You said the family was rich. Rich people are Episcopalians."

"That right? I'm sure the Kennedys would be very interested to hear that. Now *you're* being dumb."

"Maybe. But you should have tried it. They would have transferred their church membership somewhere."

Natalie sighed again. "You're right. I could have asked at all the churches."

"Or," said Paul.

"Or what?"

"Or you could have gone to see some of her old high school teachers," he said. "You had their names right there, in the yearbook. They might have known where she went."

She shook her head. "Couldn't. I thought of it. But they would have recognized me, Paul. They would have known. And I couldn't do that to her, to Julie, wherever she is."

He nodded, chewed on a blade of grass, and thought.

"Or," he said again.

She waited.

"The school," he mused. "She would have transferred to another school. They would have the records."

"I thought of that, dummy. And I called the school before I left Simmons' Mills. But it was closed. There was no one there. It was the end of June."

"So now it's the middle of July. You're not going to find her by sitting around here on your fat rear."

Natalie grabbed him around the waist and tickled him.

He pulled her to the ground and they rolled like puppies, laughing, until he had her pinned, gasping and pleading for mercy.

"Paul," she said suddenly. "Why are you trying to help, anyway? You said the whole thing was a dumb idea."

He let her go and sank to the grass again beside her. "I don't know. I guess it begins to take on the feeling of a detective story, and that appeals to me. I keep forgetting what the purpose of it is, when I start thinking about the *ways* you can do it."

"You know something funny, Paul?"

"What?"

"When I was there, and when I found out who she was, and how young she was, and especially when I saw how much she looked like me, it was weird. I mean, there I was, in her town, at her *house*, even, and I began to feel as if it was *me*. I could picture myself, there, as if I was Julie Jeffries, as if I was Cleopatra with the makeup, all of that."

He looked at her, thinking. "Yeah. I can see what you mean."

"And you know, at first, when I first found out, I was mad at her, a little. For getting pregnant. But then, after a while, when I was feeling what it felt like to *be* her, I started feeling, oh, kind of scared, and sad, the way she must have."

"God, in a small town like that, it must have been horrible for her."

"I can't figure out why she did it."

Paul laughed shortly. "You're crazy, Nat. Why does anyone do it? Because they care about another person, and they get carried away."

"That's stupid."

"Happens all the time."

"Doesn't happen to me. Or you."

"Don't kid yourself, Natalie," Paul said. "You know, a minute ago, when we were wrestling — well, you don't think I care that much about *wrestling*, do you?"

Natalie grinned at him. "Yeah," she said. "I thought you were really into it as a classical art."

"Like hell," said Paul. "I couldn't care less about wrestling and you know it. I just like touching you. Quit acting so innocent." He grabbed at her playfully again.

"Cut it out." Natalie laughed, pushing him away.

"Thwarted again." Paul groaned, broke off a fresh long blade of grass, stuck it between his teeth, and chewed on the end. "Well, anyway. You get the point."

"Julie Jeffries was a wrestler?"

"She was a human. We all are."

They watched the sky silently.

"Or—" Paul looked at her suddenly. "Listen, Nat! Call the mill! The hell with all that other stuff! They'll know, at the mill, where her family went!"

| 23 | THE PERSONNEL OFFICE at the P. R. Simmons Paper Company was not open on Saturday. The switchboard operator said politely that it would not be open until Monday. |

On Monday, Natalie had to work. On Tuesday and Wednesday, and on Thursday morning, Natalie had to work. On Thursday afternoon, she looked at the telephone, and she looked at her mother, who was trying to measure the entire house for new carpeting with a twelve-inch ruler from Nancy's geometry class.

"The width of the dining room," announced Kay Armstrong dubiously from a kneeling position, "is either twelve feet and four inches, or it's a few inches more than that, or a few inches less."

"Mom," said Natalie, "why don't you buy one of those metal measuring tapes that you pull out of a holder?"

But her mother wasn't listening. She was moving the ruler across the dining room again, muttering, trying to get the measurement right.

Natalie couldn't make the phone call with her mother in the house. In the weeks since graduation, her parents had not asked about the search for her natural parents; they had seen her off on the trip to Simmons' Mills, had welcomed her back, without asking her destination. In the beginning, they had told her that it didn't matter — not to them — what she found. If, someday, she wanted to tell them, they would listen.

And she was not ready, yet, to tell them anything.

"Natalie?" called Kay Armstrong from the dining room floor. "How tall are you?"

"Five-eight," Natalie called back from the kitchen. "Why?"

"Well, if you were six-two, two of you would be twelve feet and four inches. You could lie down twice across the dining room and I could tell if I'd measured it right."

"If I were six-two, I'd be outside playing basketball!"

"Come here a minute, Nat. Lie down here with your

feet against the wall, and I'll make a mark, and then lie down with your feet against the *other* wall, and I'll make a mark. Then I'll measure the part in the middle. It should be just one foot, if I've figured properly."

"*Mother*. Get in the car. Go to the hardware store. Buy a metal measuring tape. Please."

Her mother stood up and grinned. "Well," she said. "Since you said 'please.'"

Kay Armstrong found her pocketbook and her car keys, and left for the hardware store. Natalie went to the phone.

"Personnel," said the impersonal female voice in Simmons' Mills.

"I wonder," said Natalie nervously, doodling with her ball-point pen on the paper beside her, "if you could give me some information about someone who used to work at the mill."

"What sort of information?"

"Well, I'm trying to locate someone. I wonder if you could tell me where he went when he left Simmons Paper Company."

"I can check and see if we have that information. How long ago was he here, and in what department did he work?"

"Well, he was there in 1959 and 1960."

"Goodness. That's way back."

"Yes, I know. I'm sorry. But it's very important that I find him. I don't know what department he worked in, but he was an executive of some sort."

"Well, that will make it easier. We do maintain files on those at the executive level. Could you give me the name, please?"

"Clement Jeffries."

"Would you hold, please?"

The phone clicked and automatic music played. Natalie cringed. She would have preferred silence; instead, she got Bach's Second Brandenburg Concerto. It was a long wait.

Finally: "I have the files here on Mr. Jeffries. Let's see. He came here in 1959 from Detroit, and he was here just one year, as you said. That's unusual. Just one year. I wonder why — oh, here it is. Yes. He went, when he left Simmons, to Philadelphia. He took a position with the Wentworth Manufacturing Company in Philadelphia. That was a long time ago, of course. Frankly, I doubt if he would still be with Wentworth. He would be past retirement age by now."

Natalie wrote it down. Wentworth Manufacturing, Philadelphia. "You don't have a home address, by any chance?"

"No, I'm sorry."

"Well, thank you very much. You've been very helpful."

Natalie poured herself a Coke, called Pennsylvania information, and got the number of the Wentworth Manufacturing Company. She went through the whole thing again with the personnel department there. No music on "hold," though.

This time it was a man, in personnel.

"Clement Jeffries, Clement Jeffries, yes, here it is. He retired in 1973. And, oh, here's — is this a relative?"

"Yes," Natalie lied. "I'm his niece. But of course I

haven't seen him in a long time. I've lost track of him. That's why —"

"Well, listen, I'm sorry to be the one to tell you this, but according to our records, Clement Jeffries died in 1974."

Natalie was silent.

"Miss?"

"Yes, I'm still here. I'm sorry. I was just surprised, of course. Do you by any chance have his home address? Do you know if his wife — his widow, I mean — still lives in Philadelphia?"

"No, I'm sorry. We don't keep that kind of information."

"I see. Well, thank —"

"Miss? Hold on a minute, would you?"

Natalie waited.

A woman's voice came to the phone. "Hello?"

"Yes?"

"You were asking about the Jeffries?"

"Yes."

"This is June O'Brien. I just happened to be here in the personnel office, and I heard Bill talking to you, and I thought perhaps I could help. I remember Clement. It's funny, I didn't know him well, and I didn't know his family, but as it happens — well, you're a relative; you must know their daughter Julie?"

"Yes," said Natalie, in a whisper.

"Well, then, you remember that Julie went to Miss Sheridan's School in Connecticut. This was a *long* time ago, of course, but my own daughter went to Miss Sheridan's, and one time she got a ride home at vacation with Julie Jeffries. I went out to their house to pick Betsy up. So I remember that it was in Glen Severn. Of course I have no idea if Mrs. Jeffries still lives there. That must have been, well, let's see, Betsy would have been sixteen or seventeen then, and my goodness, she has five children *now*, so you can imagine —"

"Could you spell Glen Severn, please?"

The woman spelled it for her. Natalie thanked her, and said goodbye.

The telephone company had no record of a Jeffries in Glen Severn, Pennsylvania.

MISS SHERIDAN's, she had written. In Connecticut. She had no idea where it was in Connecticut. Or whether anyone would be there in July. Natalie called the Branford Public Library; they checked their reference books, and located Miss Sheridan's for her, in Westgarden, Connecticut. Information gave her the number.

She poured another Coke, took off her shoes, stretched her feet, and dialed Miss Sheridan's with the fingers on her other hand crossed.

"Miss Sheridan's School, hello." Funny, the change in inflections, Natalie thought. Miss Sheridan's must be a classy place. The woman put three syllables into "hello."

She went through the lies again. Looking for a cousin she'd lost track of. Julie Jeffries. Would have graduated in, oh, probably 1962.

The woman was cheerful and friendly. "Well," she said, "you've called the right person. I'm the alumnae secretary. Just a moment, please. I'll check."

A long moment. Natalie sipped her Coke and drew faces

on her paper, girls' faces with long dark hair and straight bangs.

"Hello there." Three syllables again. "Yes, I have it here. Julie Jeffries. I got out the 1962 yearbook, too, so that I could look her up. She *did* graduate that year. Goodness, wasn't she a pretty thing? It says under her picture that her ambition was to be a model."

The woman chuckled. "That's unusual, for girls from Miss Sheridan's. I wonder if she succeeded.

"I'm terribly sorry, though, that we have no current address for her. She simply hasn't responded to any of our alumnae mailings. Some girls just don't, you know. They marry, or take a job, and lose interest —"

"What's the last address you have?"

"Let me see. That would be Glen Severn, Pennsylvania. Perhaps her family still lives there, and you could call them?"

Natalie sighed, thanked her, and hung up.

She sat by the telephone for a long time, idly filling in spaces on the paper with circles and lines. You get *almost* there, she thought, frustrated, and then you're not there at all, like one of those dreams where you're running after something that keeps getting farther and farther away.

I should just give up. I don't know what else to try. She doesn't *want* to be found.

Dumb, Paul had said. You should have tried the church.

Well, thought Natalie, when in doubt or trouble, turn to the church. She called information again, in Glen Severn, Pennsylvania, and got the number of the town's only Episcopal church.

"Saint Bartholomew's," came the pleasant greeting. (Need a prayer? thought Natalie. Or a hymn? Short sermon, perhaps? How about a *mother*, long lost?)

She launched into her playscript of lies. Their name was Jeffries. I'm not even positive they were Episcopalians, but I thought perhaps —

The woman interrupted her suddenly. "Oh, you're talking about *Margaret*! Goodness, I got a card from her the other day! What a coincidence! Let's see, it's right here on my desk — Do you want her address, or her phone number, or both?"

Natalie gulped. "Let me make sure it's the right person, please. This is Mrs. Clement Jeffries —"

"Yes, I know, dear. We've been friends for a *long* time. Oh, I hated to see her move away. Goodness, Julie was *married* in this church. But you know, when Clement died, Margaret just —"

"Oh, wait. I'm sorry to interrupt you. But actually, it's Julie that I'm looking for. Do you by any chance —"

"Oh, I'm sorry. I *don't* have Julie's address. But here, I'll tell you how to reach Margaret, and then she can tell you how to get in touch with Julie."

"Thank you." Natalie picked up her pen again, and wrote it down carefully as the woman spoke. Margaret Jeffries was back in Detroit. Back where she had lived before they came to Simmons' Mills. Before they had brought Julie to Simmons' Mills to live. Before Julie . . .

She wrote it down, drew a box around it, drew arrows pointing to the box, thanked the woman, hung up, looked at the name Margaret Jeffries, realized it was her own grandmother, burst into tears, and couldn't pick up the telephone again.

24

THE PHONE RANG in the kitchen while they were at dinner, and Dr. Armstrong sighed. "I'm not on call this weekend. I'm going to watch television tonight. It *can't* be for me."

"Not for me," said Nancy, with her mouth full. "Steve's mad at me, and I just talked to Debbie, and —"

"*I'll* get it," said Kay Armstrong, putting down her fork. "And whoever it's for owes me a *big* favor."

They could hear her soft voice in the kitchen, talking for a long time. Then the resolute click of the receiver being replaced. Then silence.

"Mom?" called Natalie. "You coming back?"

Her mother returned to the dining room, pale, walking as a blind person does, carefully, through familiar places, without seeing. She sat back down.

"It's Tallie," she said, in a voice small as a child's. "I don't know, I never thought —"

She took a deep breath. "It's such a surprise. I just always thought of Tallie as — oh, Alden, she's very ill. That was a doctor in Bar Harbor.

"Let me try to remember exactly what he said. It was such a shock. *Tallie*.

"The doctor's name was Baldwin. Stan Baldwin. He says he knows you, Alden."

Dr. Armstrong nodded. "He's a good man. What did he say about Tallie?"

"She has pneumonia. Fortunately she had enough sense to call for help — I'm so glad we made her put that phone in, Alden. Just imagine, if —" She shuddered. "Well, anyway, Sonny went to the island and brought her over to Bar Harbor, to the hospital. Dr. Baldwin said they've done X-rays, and blood tests, and that she has lobar pneumonia, in both lungs. How bad is that, Alden?"

"It can be very serious, Kay. But she's in a good hospital, with a good doctor. What else did he say?"

"Not much. Her temperature is down, some, from what it was. They've started fluids intravenously, and penicillin. She asked, of course, that he not bother us. But I told him I'd come."

"I'll take you, Mom," said Natalie quickly.

Kay Armstrong looked around uncertainly. "Nancy, can you and Dad manage? Oh, that's silly. Of *course* you can. Thank you, Nat. We can leave first thing in the morning and be there by noon."

"How did she seem, when you saw her last month, Natalie?" asked her father.

Natalie smiled. "She was great, Dad. Very well, and strong. We went swimming, even, in that icy water. She said that any year now she'll be a glamorous old lady. But she sure didn't seem like an old lady when I was there."

Now, in the hospital bed, Tallie did look old. And small. There is something about hospital beds, thought Natalie, that shrinks people. It isn't fair, to diminish them like that.

But chagrin expanded Tallie. "I feel so foolish," she said weakly, taking their hands in hers. "And I hate it that you had to come all this way to see me like *this*. But I confess that I'm glad you came. I feel better already, just seeing the two of you."

"Don't talk, Tallie," said Kay, smoothing her mother's hair. "Just rest. I'm going to find Dr. Baldwin, and talk to him. Nat, you stay here and keep her company, but don't let her talk, okay?" She left the room.

"How's it going, Natalie?" asked Tallie when they were alone. "I've been so curious. I was hoping you'd write."

"Shhhh," said Natalie. "Mom said not to talk."

"Oh, hell," said Tallie. "I'm beginning to feel better already, now that I have something to interest me. You can't imagine how boring a hospital is. And *tacky*. Will you look, Natalie, at these hideous green walls? Now tell me what's going on with you?"

Natalie sat down. "Well, it's been strange, Tallie. I made this very long trip, to the town where I was born. And I found out lots of things — about the town, about my mother. Her name was Julie."

Tallie raised an eyebrow. "Not bad, for a name. Bet she was beautiful, too."

Natalie smiled. "I saw pictures of her, Tallie. She looked like me, but she was different. She *was* very beautiful — I don't mean to sound conceited, after saying she looked like me."

Tallie laughed. "Don't be silly. How was she different?"

Natalie pondered. "It's hard to say. I haven't figured it out myself. But there was something about her that didn't fit into the small town. She was smiling, in most of the pictures, but something was wrong."

"She was pregnant." Tallie chuckled. "Of course something was wrong."

"No." Natalie shook her head slowly. "Before that. I could see it in the pictures. She wasn't like the other girls, the ones she went to school with, the ones who lived in the town. Even before she became pregnant."

"Where is she now?" Tallie's eyes were bright with interest.

Natalie sighed. "I don't know. She left, after I was born. Her whole family moved away. I can find out where she is, I think, just by making a phone call, but I haven't been able to bring myself to make it. I'm not sure why. Suddenly I'm not sure that I want to intrude on her life."

Tallie rested, thinking. "You know, Nat," she said finally, "if you don't do it now, after getting this far, you'll regret it."

"I know that. But it's as if — well, I've grown to like her, Tallie."

"Surely you're not afraid that you'll like her better than your own parents?"

Natalie laughed. "No, it's not that. To be honest, I don't even think of her as my mother. I think of her as — this is really strange, Tallie —"

"You think of her as yourself. That's not strange at all. But you don't want to be disappointed."

"Yes. I guess that's really it."

"Natalie, go find her. Even if you're disappointed, you won't be sorry. I, Tallie Chandler, guarantee it."

Natalie sat quietly for a minute, and then nodded. "Okay. And you, Tallie, you take care of yourself. You're going to be all better soon. I, Natalie Armstrong, guarantee *that*."

They grinned at each other.

Natalie and her mother stayed four days in Bar Harbor. Tallie grew increasingly stronger; Dr. Baldwin said on the fourth day that her lungs were completely clear, and that she'd been afebrile for twenty-four hours.

"What does that mean?" asked Natalie.

"It means she has no fever. That she's well," said Dr. Baldwin. "She's a tough lady. But she's going to be very weak for a while. She can't go back alone to that island. Could you take her home with you, to Branford, for a while?"

"She wouldn't go," Natalie and her mother said, in unison.

"I know it." Dr. Baldwin laughed. "I thought I'd suggest it anyway. But she's done nothing for two days except talk about how soon she can get back to the island. Seems the blueberries are almost ready for picking."

"Well," said Kay Armstrong slowly, "I haven't picked blueberries for years. I'll go with her, and stay for a while. What do you think, Nat? You girls can manage at home, can't you? Keep Dad fed?"

Natalie nodded.

When she had settled her mother and grandmother together in the island house, with promises from them both that they would call if there were any problems, she drove back to Branford alone.

25 MANAGING THE HOUSE, Natalie found, was not as easy as her mother had already made it seem. Nancy helped; or Nancy *promised* cheerfully to help, and announced, just as cheerfully, when Natalie arrived home from work to find the breakfast dishes unwashed and the meat for dinner still frozen solid in the freezer, "I forgot."

"How can you *forget* that we have to eat dinner?" Natalie asked angrily.

"Well, I was babysitting at the Kimballs," Nancy replied airily. "I'm not *used* to being a domestic servant."

Natalie's feet hurt from standing most of the day in the office lab. "Well, you might as well get used to it," she said. "I'm not going to do everything myself."

We're both spoiled rotten, she realized, watching Nancy load the dishwasher halfheartedly. Mom always made everything seem easy and fun. And it *isn't*. All those dirty clothes in the hamper every morning. I didn't even realize that Nancy and I owned so many clothes. And *Dad*. He's worse than either of us. I never noticed before that he leaves his pajamas on the bedroom floor every morning. How does Mom stand it?

"Is everything running smoothly there?" asked Kay Armstrong on the telephone and didn't wait for an answer. "Tallie and I are having such fun together. We went out this morning and picked berries, and then I made pies while she rested this afternoon. Tonight we're going to have blueberry pie and tea while we listen to the symphony."

"We're all fine, Mom," said Natalie. "I don't know what we'll be doing tonight —" (Yes, I do. Last night's dishes, and yesterday's laundry) "but we'll be thinking of you. Give Tallie a hug from me."

"I will. Is Nancy there?"

"No, she went to the library with Steve." (And if she doesn't get home by nine, to help fold the clean laundry, I'll wring her neck.)

"Well, I'm glad things are going well. I think I'll be here a couple more weeks. You'll call if you have problems, won't you, Nat?"

"Sure, Mom. Just enjoy yourself, and take care of Tallie."

On Thursday afternoon, Natalie made a list and hung it on the kitchen wall.

TO WHOM IT MAY CONCERN

Will each of you please put your breakfast dishes in the dishwasher every morning?

And fold your pajamas when you get up, and make your bed?

And put milk back in the refrigerator when you're finished with it.

And be on time to meals or else call.

Good grief, she thought suddenly. I'm turning into a compulsive, list-making grouch. One of the things I always appreciated most about Mom when we were kids was that there was never a list in our house, with "Chores" written at the top. We never had to make a check mark after we cleared the table, the way my friends did.

(Of course, we never cleared the table much, either.)

Funny, because, knowing Tallie, I know there were never lists in her house, marked "Chores," either. Probably Mom never cleared the table very often when *she* was a kid. And now *we* don't. We pass our flaws and failings along from one generation to the next. Thank God we pass the good things along, too, she thought, recalling with satisfaction the spontaneity and cheer that had always been part of their home: the legacy that had been Tallie's to her daughter and that was Kay Armstrong's gift to their family now.

I wonder what Julie's mother was like, Natalie thought suddenly.

And went to the phone to call Margaret Jeffries.

26 THE VOICE FROM Michigan was clear through the telephone, all the way to Maine: clear, pleasant, and surprised, as Natalie embarked on a new sequence of explanations and lies.

"Mrs. Jeffries, you don't know me, but I was an old friend of Julie's when she was a student at Miss Sheridan's. I'd like to get in touch with her, if you could give me her address."

"Goodness; you haven't seen her in all these years?"

"No," said Natalie, hoping that her voice sounded mature. Sometimes her father's patients were surprised, when they realized she was only seventeen, after they had talked to her on the office telephone. They said she sounded older. "We just lost touch, after we graduated."

Mrs. Jeffries laughed. "Well, you *have* seen her, of course."

"No," said Natalie again, puzzled.

"I mean in magazines," said Mrs. Jeffries.

Natalie was silent for a moment. "I don't understand. Do you mean that she did become a model? I remember that she wanted to."

"Oh, my, yes. I'm amazed that you don't know that. She was so well known for a while. Goodness, there was a time when I couldn't pass a newsstand without seeing Julie's face."

"No," said Natalie slowly. "I didn't know that. I guess I just never saw her picture. Or never noticed."

"Oh, you must have seen it and not noticed. She was in — let's see — *Vogue*, *Harper's Bazaar*, on the cover of *Mademoiselle* twice, I think it was, and —"

Natalie sat down on the floor beside the telephone table and half-listened as Mrs. Jeffries went on and on, recalling Julie's professional triumphs. When I was a child, Natalie thought, I may have seen my own mother's face. She may have been on the cover of a magazine that lay on our coffee table, or in Dad's waiting room. And I never *knew*. She was right there, in my own life, and I didn't know.

"— and I was always so glad, you know, that she chose not to accept any jobs for those, you know, those magazines for *men*. She *could* have. They offered her a lot of money, some of them, if she would — well —"

"Yes," said Natalie, smiling. "I know."

"She *still* models occasionally. But of course now she's so busy with the children."

"The children?"

"Oh, yes," said Mrs. Jeffries proudly. "I have two grandsons. Gareth is six, and Cameron just had his fourth birthday last month. I made him a sweater, and then of course I sent some toys, too. Little boys don't like to get clothes for their birthday. So I —"

I have brothers, Natalie thought, as the woman talked on. Brothers. What would they be, half-brothers? Unless we have the same father. Unless Julie married the boy who was my father.

"Mrs. Jeffries," she interrupted, "could you tell me her married name, please, and her address?"

"Oh, of course," said Mrs. Jeffries. "Goodness, I was getting carried away, wasn't I? Her name is Julie Hutchinson, now. Are you writing this down? It's Mrs. E. Phillips Hutchinson. There's an *s* at the end of Phillips. It's a family name. Julie calls him Phil, of course."

"Of course." Natalie had written the name down, and drawn a circle around it. Her small notebook was filled, now, with hastily written names, phone numbers, addresses, and designs drawn in frustration in the margins. Clues. Dead ends. And now, the name Mrs. E. Phillips Hutchinson. She drew another circle and two exclamation points.

Mrs. Jeffries gave her the address, on East 79th Street, in New York, and Natalie wrote that carefully, below the name.

New York. It was a long way from Simmons' Mills.

"I'd love to talk longer, dear, but I'm going to be late for a bridge game. Give Julie my love when you see her, won't you? I'm so glad you called."

So am I, thought Natalie, after she had hung up the phone. She looked for a long time at the name in her notebook. In her mind, the picture she had had of the frightened, dark-haired fifteen-year-old-girl had changed to that of a mature, self-assured, beautiful woman. A mother. (Again. Still.)

The back door banged, and Nancy came into the kitchen, carrying a tennis racquet. Her hair damp and curly, the freckles across her nose dark against her tan.

"I beat Steve," she announced, grinning. "Two sets. He's furious. Why are you sitting on the floor looking silly?"

"Nancy," said Natalie, grinning back. "Old buddy. This weekend, *you* are going to do the cooking. The dishes. The laundry. All that neat stuff."

Nancy shrugged. "Okay. Big deal. How come?"

Natalie took a deep breath. "Because *I*," she said, "am going to New York."

27 NEW YORK WAS new to Natalie. She had never been there before. Early August heat rose from the sidewalks in shimmers; taxis were honking yellow clusters at every corner; pedestrians were perspiring and quick-tempered.

Thank God, thought Natalie, as she stood holding her suitcase on the street corner where the cab from the airport had dropped her, that I didn't try to drive here. I would never have made it. I would have had a nervous break-down. I would simply have stopped my car somewhere, in the middle of one of these streets, and cried.

Near her, waiting for a light, holding tightly to her mother's hand, a small girl in a flowered dress *was* crying. "You're making me miss all my prooograms," she wailed.

"Hush," said her mother shortly. "You'll love the museum."

"I *hate* museums," the child whimpered. As the light changed, taxis came to abrupt and squealing halts, and her mother shook her loose from her determined stance and started across the street.

Natalie looked up. Around her, the tall buildings coalesced in distorted, dizzying perspective against the sky and reflected the heat from their acres of glass windows. No one else was looking up at all. The crowds surged past, looking straight ahead. Three men in business suits were speaking what seemed to be Russian. A tall black woman, her head completely shaved, moved by Natalie languidly, walking a small dog on the end of a leash.

On the other side of Fifth Avenue, the southern end of Central Park was a green and gold interruption in the steel and concrete city, as if a smile had appeared unexpectedly on the countenance of a statue. The park was busy on this hot Friday; from where she stood, in front of the hotel, Natalie could hear the shrieks of exuberant children, the whispered whir of bicycles, the short barks of small, leashed dogs, and the measured clop of the straw-hatted horses who pulled hansom cabs of tourists slowly along the street, oblivious to the taxis, buses, and crowds.

"Miss?" The uniformed doorman was reaching for her suitcase with a questioning smile.

"Thank you," said Natalie, and followed him into the hotel.

She had chosen it from the New York directory in Branford's library, which had told her that it was close to Julie Hutchinson's apartment. It had not told her the price. Now she winced inwardly, realizing she had reserved a room in one of Manhattan's finest old hotels, and that it was not going to be, as Anna Talbot's had been, seven dollars for the night. "And that includes breakfast, dear."

Here, she would be lucky to get the breakfast, alone, for seven dollars.

Natalie felt a surge of gratitude for her father's generosity, for the checking account he had provided to finance a project he didn't understand.

She followed the doorman up the short, carpeted stairs.

Past the small fountain surrounded by flowering plants.

Under the crystal chandeliers that dangled like diamond earrings from the high, carved ceiling.

Past the two women speaking in French to a petulant poodle.

Into the cool, impersonal hush. Here, in contrast to the heat and vibrant life of the park, things were subdued, efficient, elegant, and layered with a dim chill.

This is a long way, thought Natalie, from Branford. An even longer way from Simmons' Mills.

After she had unpacked her small suitcase in the spacious room, and watched for a moment the unceasing activity in the park from her window, she took the elevator down, again, to the lobby, and approached the registration desk and the brisk, tastefully dressed woman who had checked her in.

"I wonder," Natalie asked shyly, "if you could tell me how to find this address." She showed the woman the card on which she had written Julie Hutchinson's address. "Is it within walking distance from here?"

"Oh, I would think so, unless you're in a hurry," the woman told her. "That would be just between Park and Madison — closer to Park. Do you know New York?"

Natalie smiled and shook her head. Can't she see the hayseeds in my hair? she thought.

"Well, you're on Fifth, now, and 65th. You want to walk north on Fifth —" she pointed — "until you get to 79th. That will be up by the Metropolitan." She looked at Natalie, expecting some kind of recognition. Natalie looked blank.

"You don't know the Metropolitan Museum of Art?"

Natalie shook her head.

"Goodness. If you have time while you're here, do stop in there. They're having a special exhibition this month, of impressionists. Here, I'll give you a brochure." The woman handed her a brochure on thick textured paper, with a reproduction, on the front, of a pastel and hazy painting of a woman holding a child.

"Now, when you get to 79th, which is up by the museum, turn right. Go one block and cross Madison, and then in the second block, almost to Park, you'll find this address."

"Thank you."

"I don't think there's any possible way that you could

get lost. But if you do, just get a taxi." The woman smiled at her.

Help, thought Natalie, suddenly panicky. Should I give her a tip? I've given everyone else a tip. The taxi driver. The doorman. The bellboy.

But the woman had turned away pleasantly and was talking to a dapper man in a pinstriped suit who wanted to know if a telegram had come for him from Oslo. Natalie made her way to the street and began walking north.

28

WELL, SHE THOUGHT. Here I am. And, as usual, not knowing what to do next.

She stood uncertainly on the wide sidewalk and looked again at the building. It was an apartment building, older than many in the neighborhood, smaller than most, and thoroughly elegant. A gray-haired doorman in a brass-buttoned green uniform stood at the doorway and spoke occasionally to the few people who entered or left. He helped a young woman in a white uniform with an English baby carriage and exchanged a few laughing remarks with her as she started off toward Central Park with her charge. Then he opened the door of an arriving taxi, took the packages marked Bonwit Teller from a middle-aged lady in a deep blue linen dress, and escorted her into the building. He looked at Natalie curiously.

I have to get out of here. If Julie Hutchinson comes out of that building, I am going to faint.

She walked slowly back toward Fifth Avenue, idly leafing through the brochure from the Metropolitan Museum. On the last page, it mentioned the hours that the museum was open and the fact that it contained a restaurant. Suddenly Natalie was very hungry. It was already two o'clock; she had left Maine early in the morning, and hadn't eaten since dawn.

She crossed Madison Avenue and headed toward Fifth and the museum. *It's nice*, she thought, *finally to have a destination. Even if it is only for lunch.*

Seated with her salad and iced tea beside the shallow pool and its tall, thin sculptured figures, she thought over her alternatives carefully.

I could go back to the apartment building and simply pay her a visit. Except that I would be too scared. And it wouldn't be fair to her, to do it without any warning. Cancel that idea.

I could go back to the hotel and call her on the phone. Except I'm scared to do that, too. How can I explain things on the phone? She might hang up on me.

I could write her a note. I should have done that before I came. But I was afraid she wouldn't answer. If I mailed it right now, she would get it tomorrow. I think. *I could ask her to call me. I could explain how far I've come. She would have a little time to think, and then she'd call.*

And if she didn't get it tomorrow? The next day is Sunday; no mail deliveries on Sundays. And I have to leave Sunday, anyway.

I can't waste this trip. I have to do *something*.

(I could sit here surrounded by sculpture and people and cry. That's what I *feel* like doing.)

Then, as quickly and clearly as one of the water drops falling from the fountains of the shallow pool, she realized what she would do.

I'll write a note, and I'll give it to the doorman in the green uniform. I'll go back to the hotel, and wait for her to call.

If she doesn't call?

She will. Because she's my mother.

There was no one waiting for tables; it was three o'clock now, and the lunch crowds had passed. Natalie got another glass of iced tea, and took from her pocketbook the stationery that she had found in her room at the hotel. It was pale gray, embossed at the top with the name and address — and phone number — of the hotel.

"Dear Mrs. Hutchinson," she wrote.

That doesn't seem right, she thought. Well, what should I say? Dear *Mother*? No way.

She took out a second sheet of paper and wrote firmly, "Dear Julie." The rest came surprisingly easily.

This will come as a surprise to you, and I hope not an unpleasant one.

My name is Natalie Armstrong. I am the child to whom you gave birth in September 1960, in Simmons' Mills.

I am now seventeen years old. For the past two months I have been trying to find you. Now finally here I am, a few blocks away from you, and I am at a loss about what I should do next.

I don't want to disrupt your own life in any way. My life, too, is a happy one.

But I want so much to see you, and to talk. Perhaps all these years you have been wondering, too, as I have.

I will be at the hotel for the rest of the afternoon and evening. Would you call me, there? Please.

Sincerely,
Natalie

She folded the paper, sealed it in the pale gray envelope, wrote "Mrs. E. Phillips Hutchinson" on the outside, left the museum, walked down the long steps, across Fifth Avenue, down to 79th Street, across Madison, and back to the apartment building. The doorman was hailing a taxi for a man and a teen-aged boy who had just come from the building.

"Excuse me," she said to him, after the taxi slid away from the curb and eased itself into the traffic.

"Yes?" He smiled.

"I have a note that I'd like delivered to Mrs. Hutchinson," said Natalie, a little nervously.

The doorman looked at his watch. "It's almost four," he said. "I believe she'll be back very soon. Would you like to wait in the lobby?"

"Oh, no," said Natalie. She took the note from her pocketbook, and gave it to him, with a dollar bill. "Please, would you just give this to her when she comes back?"

"Certainly," he said. "Anything else?"

"Yes," replied Natalie, suddenly exhausted. "Would you get me a taxi, please?"

The streets were a blur as she sank against the creased, scarred leather of the taxi seat. Now, she thought, I'll have to rehearse what I'm going to say.

But there wasn't time. She had barely entered her room at the hotel and taken off her shoes, when the phone rang. Natalie's stomach lurched as if she were on the top of a ferris wheel, at the place where you begin to slide over into the downward curve, and the ground disappears for a moment, so that you hang in space and feel for an instant as if you will fall. She took a deep breath, cleared her throat, and picked up the phone on the third ring.

"Hello?" Natalie said.

"Natalie? This is Julie Hutchinson."

The voice was uncertain, soft, carefully modulated, sophisticated, and friendly. Oh, thank you, thought Natalie. Thank you for the friendliness. Tears formed in her eyes and fell on her cheeks, released in a surge from the tentative bondage that had held them there somewhere in her head all day.

"Yes, this is Natalie. Oh, I'm sorry —" she said, realizing that the tears were obvious in her voice. "It's just that —"

"I know. I know. It's all right." There was a sudden shakiness to Julie's voice, as well.

"I'm okay," said Natalie, wiping her face with the back of her hand, like a small child. "I just didn't know if you would call at all, and I didn't know what I would say if you did, and —"

"Natalie. That's a lovely name."

"Thank you. It's my grandmother's name but no one ever calls her that. Everyone calls my grandmother Tallie;

they always have, and —" I'm babbling, thought Natalie, embarrassed.

"You know, I saw your taxi leaving. My own pulled up just behind yours, and when George gave me your note, he pointed and said that you had just left."

"I didn't want to see you. He said you'd be back soon, and I didn't want to take you by surprise like that."

"Thank you. Your note, in itself, was a surprise, of course. In fact, I've been sitting here reading it again and again. But, Natalie, it never occurred to me *not* to call."

"I'm so glad," Natalie whispered.

"I confess I'm at a complete loss. I have no idea how you *ever* found me. Do you live in New York? Of course not; you're at the hotel. Where have you come from?"

"Maine," said Natalie. "I've never left Maine. I've lived there all my life."

She could hear Julie sigh.

"Natalie, it was such a long, long time ago. But I *have* wondered. For years, I've wondered. I don't know if you realize this, but when you were born, I was just — well, I was only —" Her voice broke.

"I know," said Natalie. "You were very young. Younger than I am now."

"And I couldn't —" Julie's voice shook. "There was just no way — I wanted to —"

"I know," said Natalie. "I understand. It doesn't matter. What matters is that *finally* I found you. And we can talk."

"Natalie," Julie said, "I don't quite know how to go about this. You can understand, can't you, that it would be a little awkward for me to invite you here?"

"Yes, of course. But I can see you, can't I?"

"How long can you stay in New York?"

"Until Sunday."

She could hear Julie thinking, in the silence.

"And you're all alone?"

"Yes."

"My goodness. Listen, Natalie, don't try to go out for dinner tonight. Not by yourself. Have dinner in the hotel. I *wish* I could invite you here, but we have company coming, and I just don't see *how* —"

"It's all right. I was planning to have dinner here, anyway."

"Well, then. Here's what we'll do. I'll meet you for lunch tomorrow. Have you ever been in New York before?"

"No. I'm overwhelmed by it."

Julie laughed. "I should think so. I was, too, once. Oh, there's so much I'd like to show you, and we won't have time. Let me see. Do you know the Russian Tea Room?"

Natalie chuckled. "I don't know *anything*."

"Of course not. I forgot for a minute. Well, take a cab tomorrow, around one, to the Russian Tea Room. That's West 57th Street, near Carnegie Hall. I'll meet you there. Now, don't try to walk or take a subway. It won't be very expensive to take a taxi, and it's much safer."

"Okay." Natalie wrote down the name of the restaurant, and the address.

"Natalie, do you need any money?"

"Oh, no. That's not a problem."

"Well, I don't know how you chose your hotel, but do

you realize it's one of the most expensive in New York?"

Natalie laughed. "Well, I didn't realize it when I made the reservation. I chose it because it seemed to be fairly near to where you lived. But as soon as I *saw* it, I knew it wasn't your local small-town motel. But it doesn't matter, Julie. I have enough money."

"You have a sense of humor, too. That's terrific. I have a feeling we may both need to laugh a lot, to get through this."

"Julie?"

"Yes?"

"Thank you for calling. I was so scared."

"I still *am*, Natalie. But you know, I'm really looking forward to seeing you. Whoops. I just thought of something."

"What?"

"How will I know you?"

Natalie was silent for a moment. Then she said, "Julie, I don't quite know how to tell you this, but —"

"But what?"

"I think I look just like you."

29 WHEN JULIE HUTCHINSON entered the Russian Tea Room, it was as if the curtain had been lifted and the actress was on stage, poised, acknowledging the hush that preceded the applause. Conversations stopped. Forks were lowered slowly to plates.

Julie stood for a moment, half-smiling, at the front of the restaurant, aware of the sudden pause, the brief silence, and then the ripple of murmurs that moved from table to table.

Natalie watched her, from the table where she had been seated, with awe, and forgot for a moment that Julie was her mother.

Julie was incredibly beautiful. She was tall, like Natalie, and very thin; her dark hair was in a stark chignon; her eyes, pale blue, were heavily adorned with mascara and eye shadow, and her eyebrows were plucked into narrow curved arches and darkened to black. She had very little visible makeup on; but Natalie, studying her, knew that her cheekbones could not be so pronounced, her lips so artfully pink, without hours in front of a mirror. She stood like a model, her slender hands graceful at her waist, as she looked around the tables. When she saw Natalie, she smiled and waved.

As she made her way toward Natalie, she smiled and mouthed greetings to countless people who called "Julie!"; she waved toward the back at a tall man who blew her a kiss; and touched the shoulder of another as she passed.

This isn't the right place to be, thought Natalie suddenly, for this meeting.

"Natalie," said Julie softly, taking her hand.

They looked at each other. "You do," said Julie finally. "You look exactly as I did when I was your age. Looking at you is like having a mirror into the past."

Natalie had dressed carefully for the lunch. She had taken a long shower at the hotel, washed her hair, and combed it thick and straight down her back. She was wearing a yellow silk dress and small silver earrings to match the necklace that Nancy had given her for graduation. Now, beside Julie, she felt dowdy, unkempt, and inarticulate.

And she felt curiously angry at Julie, who made her feel that way.

Julie ordered for them both. The waiter called her Mrs. Hutchinson, with his heavy Slavic accent, and she told him her selections in Russian. Then she waved greetings to a shaggy-haired man in theatrical makeup who had joined a group at a nearby table.

"Now," she said, turning to Natalie. "We must talk and talk. There is so much to catch up on, isn't there? First I want to know *how* you found me."

It was hard to remember, suddenly. Natalie told her slowly about the trip to Simmons' Mills. About Anna Talbot. The librarian. Foster Goodwin, who was dead.

Julie made a face. "I hated Foster Goodwin," she said. "In fact, I hated that town and almost everything about it. My house — did you see my house?"

"Yes. I drove up Falls Road. The woman who lives there let me go up the driveway and see the front. I didn't go inside."

Julie frowned. "When I moved to Simmons' Mills, I loved that house. It was so sort of Gothic, mysterious, glamorous. I thought maybe it would be fun living there after all, even though I'd hated leaving Detroit. But then as it turned out, the house set me apart from the other kids in the town. Being up on the hill. I never, in the time I lived there — it was only for my sophomore year in high school — really felt part of the town. It was my fault as much as the town's, of course."

Lunch had come. Julie picked up her fork and touched the food on her plate absently. "So Foster Goodwin's dead. I remember the day he came to the hospital, with those papers. If I could have killed him myself, right then, I would have. But of course he was only doing what he had to do. He was right, of course. Doc Therrian had told me the same thing. Did you see him? Now *there* was a man I loved. Please don't tell me that he's gone, too."

"I was getting to that. It was Dr. Therrian who told me who you were, Julie. He's very sick. I went to the hospital to see him, and Julie, when I went in, he thought I was you."

"I'm not surprised. He and I were very close, and you look so much as I did, then."

Natalie told her of the phone calls that had led, finally, to Margaret Jeffries in Detroit. Julie smiled.

"Mother's so proud of me. And her grandchildren. Did she tell you I have two little boys?"

Natalie nodded. And me, she thought. You have me, too.

"Somehow," Julie said, "she finally managed to put that whole incident at Simmons' Mills out of her mind. I really think she's forgotten about it. It was very hard on her and Daddy. They were angry, and embarrassed. If it hadn't been for Doc Therrian, who was so terribly kind to me — well."

"Julie," said Natalie. "I'd really like it if you could tell me what happened. And what you were like, then. So I could understand it all better."

Julie nodded and took a bite of salad. Natalie noticed the way she ate, carefully, in tiny bites, so that she wouldn't mar the perfectly applied pink lipstick.

"I will. But first I want to hear about you, Natalie. Tell me about your life."

Natalie laughed. "My life? It's so ordinary, compared to yours. My parents went to Simmons' Mills, to Foster Goodwin's office, to get me when I was five days old. I suppose you were just leaving the hospital then."

Julie made a face. "I sure was. Back to Falls Road, where no one spoke about it at all. And then whisked off to boarding school a few weeks later. When I went to Miss Sheridan's, for my junior year, I arrived late, and the story was that I'd 'been traveling.' Some trip. To the Simmons' Mills delivery room."

She sounded bitter.

"Well," Natalie went on, after a moment, "my family lives in Branford, down near Portland. My dad's a doctor. Funny thing, after they adopted me, a few months later, my mother became pregnant. I guess that happens often; someone who can't have a baby suddenly has one after they adopt the first."

"I wouldn't know," said Julie. "Infertility has not been one of my problems."

Please don't, thought Natalie. Don't sound angry about *me*. None of this was *my* fault.

"So I have a sister," she said finally. "Nancy. She's terrific. What else can I tell you? I graduated from high school this spring, and next month I'll start at MacKenzie College. I'm going to be a doctor, like my dad."

Julie was looking at her with new interest. "Pull your hair back a minute, Natalie."

Natalie put down her fork, and held her hair behind her head.

"You know," said Julie, "you could be a model! I mean, really, Natalie, you have the same facial bones I have, and the same eyes. That's what made me successful. I've really gotten too old, now, or will soon. I'm thirty-three; *imagine*. But, Natalie, ten years ago, even five years ago, you wouldn't believe the *money* I was making. It was an incredible life. Hard work. But you're not afraid of hard work, are you?"

Natalie shook her head. "No, but — "

"If you'd let me take you to a salon where they'd restyle your hair. And then I could advise you on how to dress and use makeup. You know, with something black on, and some very elegant, clunky jewelry. Well, look, that necklace you're wearing; it's cute, you know, but, really — "

Natalie put her hand protectively around the silver necklace that was Nancy's gift. Don't, she thought.

Julie was talking on and on. "You can't imagine the feeling, Natalie, of having your face on the covers of magazines. Walking into parties and having everyone turn to look at you. They used to say 'Julie Jeffries' in whispers when I entered a room. They could do that to you. What's your last name? I've forgotten."

"Armstrong," said Natalie.

Julie frowned. "Well, I think you'd want to change that. The first name is nice. You could even call yourself

Natalia; you know, make it a little more exotic, and then think up a last name with a little foreign flavor to it. Or maybe no last name at all! Just: *Natalia*."

Stop it, thought Natalie angrily. Don't take my name away from me. You did that once, already.

"Thank you, Julie," she said aloud. "But I really want to be a doctor. I guess I won't have as glamorous a life, or make as much money, but it's what I want."

"Oh," said Julie, surprised, her hand fluttering in a gesture. "I see. Well, if you should change your mind."

The waiter took their plates, and brought tea. Julie glanced at the platinum watch on her wrist.

"Darling, I'm going to have to dash. It's been such *fun*, seeing you. And I've brought you something. You asked what I was like, when I was your age. I'm not at all sure it's something I want to remember, but for some reason I've kept this all these years. It's the little diary I kept that year in Simmons' Mills. You read it if you want to, and I think it will answer all your questions. Then — when do you have to go back?"

"Tomorrow. My plane leaves at five."

"Well, then, why don't you come on over to the apartment around two? Phil will be gone for the afternoon. The children will be there, but their nurse keeps them out of the way. We'll have tea."

"All right. Thank you." Natalie took the small blue leather book that Julie had removed from her purse.

"I'm afraid you'll find it very immature and sad," Julie said, laughing lightly.

"I suppose you were," answered Natalie. "Immature and sad."

140

"What?" Julie looked startled. She wiped her lips carefully with her napkin and gathered her pocketbook and the bill for the lunch. "Oh. Yes. Goodness, I guess you're right. I certainly was. Bye, love. I'll see you tomorrow, then."

And she was gone, in a flurry of waves across the restaurant again. Natalie sat at the table alone for a moment, holding the small blue book on her lap.

Then she left the Russian Tea Room, disregarded Julie's advice about taxis, and walked all the way back to the hotel. The streets were clearly marked, and she had no trouble finding her way from the west side of Manhattan to the east, over to Fifth Avenue, and north to Central Park. The city crowds surged around her; occasionally someone glanced at her with an appraising admiration, and she was aware that she did have Julie's eyes, Julie's face; that she was, or could be, as beautiful as Julie.

Ahead of her she saw her hotel, familiar now, and felt some satisfaction that she had found the way alone. But at the same time she had never felt so completely, so painfully, lost.

THE HANDWRITING (Natalie smiled) was like Nancy's: round, cute, with circles instead of dots over the i's. Young.

The diary, with a page designated for each day, was like all such diaries, like those she had kept herself when she was younger; she remembered writing on an inside cover once: NANCY ARMSTRONG YOU RAT YOU KEEP YOUR NOSE OUT OF THIS BOOK. Julie's diary had no such admonitions; but there were the same blank pages, as when you didn't bother writing, or forgot. The days when you wrote in large handwriting, because nothing much had happened but you wanted to fill the page anyway; and the occasional day when so much had taken place that you ran over the page into the next day's date. The things that seemed so important and private when you were fourteen; and later, when you reread them, seemed no more than the secrets of all children.

Julie's secrets, Natalie knew, would be more painful, more private ones than her own had ever been. But she saw when she flipped the pages that Julie's method of keeping a journal had been much like her own.

October 10th. (The printed January 1st crossed out in green ink, and carefully relettered with the correct date.)
I hate it here. There is nothing — NOTHING — to do, and everyone hates me anyway. It's because of the socks. In Detroit we wore our socks *up*, and here they wear them *down*. Everyone laughed when I came into homeroom the first day with my socks up. How was I supposed to know? And I'm way behind in Geometry, too. There's a cute boy in homeroom, but he was one of the ones who laughed loudest at my socks.

October 15th.
If I ever get it all straight, I think things will be okay. Socks down (it feels so stupid, that way). Pony tails are out. I have to wear my hair down all the time. You tuck the baggy part of

your gym suit under, and embroider your name on the back with that thread that turns into different colors. Some of the kids are nice. I'm trying out for cheerleader. And the house is really neat. My room is painted blue. Mom's making plaid curtains for it.

October 22nd.
I made it! Cheerleader! I didn't think I would, because I was new, but no one else could do a back flip. Margo and Anne invited me to go to the movies Friday.

November 1st.
I can't believe how cold it is here. And it will get worse. It snowed Thursday and there was no school. Mom and I made cookies. The house is so far up the hill and away from town that the other kids can't ever come over. I washed my hair and put it in pin curls, but it looks awful, curly. Margo has natural curls, and says she wishes hers was straight, like mine.

November 10th.
Tryouts for "Caesar and Cleopatra." I think I'll get Cleopatra because my hair is right. I'll never remember the lines, though.

November 15th.
They announced the play parts, and I did get Cleopatra. Tony Gearhart is Caesar. Ugh. I hate him.

November 16th.
Margo said that Tony told someone he wishes he didn't get the part because he doesn't like me. Because I'm *affected*. What's that supposed to mean? That I don't have a Maine accent? I can't help it. He wouldn't go over too big in Detroit, either.

November 19th.

Well. No one asked me to the Thanksgiving dance. Everyone in the whole school is going, I think, except me. I can't figure it out. The teachers all like me. Margo likes me, I think. Practically everyone else acts as if they're *scared* of me. Margo says the other girls are jealous because I'm pretty. What do they have to be jealous of, when the boys don't like me, either? I hate this town so. I'd give anything to be back in Detroit.

November 22nd.

Thanksgiving vacation. Everyone is going skiing. I'm the only one in the whole school who doesn't know how to ski. I'll probably read twelve books over the long weekend. Margo said the dance was great. Who cares.

November 23rd.

I met the neatest guy at the library. His name is Terry and he's home from Dartmouth on vacation. He bought me a Coke at the drugstore and asked me to go to the movies tomorrow night. Mom and Dad say they have to think it over because he's so much older. Big deal. He's twenty. What difference does five years make? Dad is three years older than Mom.

November 24th.

They let me go and I had the neatest time. Terry has a car. The movie was dumb, but afterward we got a Coke and talked for a long time. Terry hates Simmons' Mills too, even though he graduated from high school here and was captain of the basketball team. Here's what he *likes*: basketball, the theater (he goes to Boston to see plays!), Captain Kangaroo (?), Sophia Loren (!), chocolate marshmallow ice cream, cashmere sweaters, and beer (!). I asked him to come to "Caesar and Cleopatra," even though I probably won't be any good. But he has to go back to Dartmouth tomorrow night. Ugh.

November 25th.
Terry came over this afternoon and we walked in the woods behind my house. I got snow in my boots. He asked me to write to him at Dartmouth! He probably won't write back. But he *did* kiss me goodbye. I mean really kissed me. You can tell he's not just a kid. School tomorrow. I hate to go back . . . What a great vacation.

December 3rd.
The play went pretty well. Tony blew a couple of lines, but I remembered all mine. Everyone said I looked terrific in my Cleopatra makeup and costume. But after it was over (I found out later) all the kids went to Tony's house, and I wasn't invited. I don't even care. I got a postcard from Terry, so now I can write back without feeling stupid.

December 8th.
Terry answered my letter right away. His letter was so much more mature than mine. I'll have to be more careful, writing. He talked about his courses. He takes Economics, Political Science, Geology, English, and Calculus. He must be a brain. And he said he went to a dance at Bennington . . . a girls' college. *Then* he said no one at Bennington was as pretty as me!

December 15th.
There's going to be a Christmas dance at school. Margo's mother is making her a new formal. No one will ask me, I know. They're all nice enough to me in school, but then when

school ends in the afternoon, it's as if I don't even exist. I sit up here in this castle on the hill and feel sorry for myself all the time. But I got another letter from Terry. He signed it "Love."

December 19th.

I can't believe it! I wrote and asked Terry if he'd be home for vacation in time for the Christmas dance on the 22nd, and he *called* to say yes! Wait'll I show up at that dumb dance with *him*. That'll put a few people in their places. It's too late to get a new dress. But I can wear the pink one I got in Detroit last spring. No one's seen it here.

December 23rd.

You should have seen their faces when Terry and I showed up. I mean you should have *seen* their faces! We got there kind of late. He came to pick me up on time, but then we sat in his car outside the school while he drank two cans of beer before we went in. I had a couple of sips. He said it would be impossible to get through a high school dance without it. I think he's probably right. But it was a great dance. A couple of other guys, high school kids, asked me to dance, but mostly I danced with Terry. You should have seen the other girls watching. He brought me a gardenia corsage. It's turning all brown at the edges, but I'm saving it anyway. We made out in the car, afterward, in my driveway, until Daddy started blinking the porch lights.

December 25th.

Mom and Daddy gave me a camera for Christmas and two cashmere sweaters . . . one yellow, one gray! Grandma and Grandpa sent money, and Aunt Sue sent me a gorgeous blouse. And I got lots of other stuff. But best of all . . . Terry gave me a silver ring with the Dartmouth crest on it! I only gave him a book of Shaw's plays, but he liked it, I could tell.

I'm wearing his ring on a chain around my neck so Mom and Daddy won't see it. They'd ask what it *means*. I don't really know what it means, because I didn't have the nerve to ask Terry that. I suppose we're engaged to be engaged, or something. I feel so much older than fifteen.

December 27th.
It's scary, sometimes, being with Terry. Like tonight, we were supposed to go to the movies. Only after we drove off from my house, he decided he didn't want to go to the movies at all. He just wanted to park. He got mad at me when I said no. He said in college, that's what everybody does. He said well, he'd just take me back home, then. So I gave in, and we drove up the River Road and parked behind the mill. I don't know what to do. I can't lose Terry because he's all I have. All the other kids are off skiing. Even if they weren't, they wouldn't call me. And of course, I love Terry. I'm quite sure of that, I think.

December 28th.
Terry called and said he was sorry about last night. We talked a long time. He said he really loves me. He wants to marry me someday, when he's finished Dartmouth (2 years!) and maybe law school (3 more years!) By then I'll be 20. That's a long time to wait. When I told him that, he said we don't have to *wait*. I am so scared by him sometimes. That's strange, to be scared by someone you are more or less engaged to. I wish there were someone I could talk to. Not my parents. They'd just die. Maybe Margo. But she's off skiing with the kids from school. I wish I had a sister. I'm so lonely sometimes.

December 30th.
My mother told me there's a party New Year's Eve at Tony Gearhart's. She asked why I wasn't going. I couldn't tell her

I wasn't invited. So I said that I was going out with Terry and that we'd probably go to the party. But the truth is that I think Terry's mad at me. I asked him yesterday about New Year's Eve, and he said his parents were going out that night, and that maybe he and I could go to his house and celebrate the arrival of 1960. I knew what he meant. I said no, I didn't want to go to his house, so he said well, maybe he'd find someone who would. But that I'm the one he really loves. I believe him, too. He gave me the ring.

Later
I called Terry and told him I would go with him, wherever he wanted to go, New Year's Eve.

January 1st, 1960.
It's a new year, and I'm all different. I don't *feel* much different. I feel strange, though. I suppose I shouldn't have gone, with Terry, to his house. Then nothing would have happened. But if I hadn't, I would have been all alone here on this hillside, feeling sorry for myself. As it was, at least I had him, and he said he loved me, even afterward, when he took me home. It was very scary, and exciting, but not the big deal that I expected. To tell the truth, I think Terry was just as scared as I was, just as much an amateur. We both felt kind of stupid afterward, and decided we wouldn't let that happen again. He's going back to Dartmouth tomorrow, anyway.

January 5th.
School again. Everything is *so* boring. I got a B on a French test. Margo said that Tim McLain likes me. He's not bad-looking.

January 18th.
Not much happening lately. I haven't heard from Terry even though I've written him twice. I saw his father at the drugstore, and he said they haven't heard from him either, and probably he's very busy getting started in the new semester. Tim is going to give me ski lessons this weekend. I'll probably make a fool of myself.

January 23rd.
Hey, I'm not bad at skiing! I bought a red knitted hat, and Tim says I look like Elizabeth Taylor. Hah.

January 24th.
I can't believe it. I just checked the calendar, and then I went back and checked last month's calendar, and I'm sure I had my period *before* the Christmas dance, so now it's overdue and I've never been late before. I *know* I can't be pregnant. At least I'm almost positive, because (1) it only happened once, and it's only in books that it only happens once and you get pregnant and (2) it was all over so *fast*, how could anything have happened to make me pregnant? and (3) Terry said he was being careful, whatever that meant.

January 26th.
Maybe I should write and tell Terry.

January 30th.
Tim took me skiing and I went up the T-bar without falling four times. Fell the fifth time, and everyone behind me tripped over me, but they all laughed, including Tim, who is very, very nice. No mail from Terry. No anything else, either. I am petrified. Maybe if I ski a lot and *fall* a lot, *hard*.

February 7th.

I can't tell my parents. I just can't.

February 20th.

I wrote to Terry and told him. No answer. Now what? Just keep skiing. Keep falling. Take hot baths. Pray.

March 1st.

Well. I suppose I've known for a long time, but now it's official. Julie Jeffries, the youngest pregnant person in Simmons' Mills, Maine.

I was so scared, and Terry didn't answer my letters, and I knew I had to do something, and I thought of killing myself, and knew that wasn't the answer. I couldn't tell my parents. Finally I happened to see Dr. Therrian on the street, and I remembered how nice he's always been to me. So I went to his office, and told him everything. I cried and cried. Bless him. He was so terrific. He examined me (ugh) and confirmed what I already knew, that I'm two months along. We talked a long time, about Simmons' Mills, and about how I had felt so lonely, and when Terry came along he and I both acted foolishly, probably for different reasons. We talked about what I should do. First, Dr. Therrian says I must tell my parents. That's rough. I'm trying to get up my nerve. Then . . . because I don't have the nerve to, or don't even want to, I guess . . . Dr. Therrian is going to call Terry at Dartmouth, and talk to him. He (Dr. T.) thinks the best thing to do is arrange to have the baby (BABY! I can't even write the word without cringing) adopted by some great family who wants a child. In the meantime, I have to take millions of vitamins and go see Dr. Therrian once a month. Or more often, if I want, just to talk. It's so good to have someone to talk to.

March 3rd.

I wonder when it will *show*. I quit cheerleading, just on general principles. And when Tim calls, I tell him I can't go out. It's crummy, missing out on fun. But I don't feel right, dating, under the circumstances. I can't get up the nerve to tell my parents.

March 5th.

I stopped to see Dr. Therrian. He had called Terry. He said Terry is sad, scared, and very immature. That it really would be best to give the baby up. I guess until he told me that, I still thought that maybe Terry and I would get married. But I don't think I wanted to.

March 10th.

I told Mom and Daddy. They both cried. They got angry. Then they said they loved me and would help me through it.

April 30th.

One more month of school, and I still don't show. I think I can make it till school ends, if I wear the right clothes. Dr. Therrian says it's because I'm tall, that sometimes tall women don't get all bulky the way others do. The baby is due in September. Mom and Daddy thought I should go away for the summer. I don't know.

May 23rd.

I've only gained nine pounds. No one knows, except me, Mom and Daddy, Dr. Therrian, and of course, Terry, but I haven't heard from him at all. Sometimes . . . this is *weird* . . . I actually like the feeling of having a baby growing. I can feel it move.

June 10th.

Thank God school is over. I'm really starting to get big. I've decided to stay here for the summer, just at home. Mom and Daddy are going to tell everyone that I've gone back to Detroit for the summer, but actually I'm just going to stay here in the house. It's private. I can sunbathe and stuff, but I won't have to see people. Doc Therrian says he'll come to the house now and then for checkups. When I have to go to the hospital, of course, the secret will be blown. The nurses there will probably tell someone. But by then it won't really matter. Mom and Daddy said I don't have to go back to school here. I can go away and start all over.

June 22nd.

Doc Therrian says I'm very, very healthy, that I will have a fine baby. It feels very strong. It kicks against my insides. I wonder if it's a boy or a girl. Funny, I can barely remember Terry at all. He went out to Colorado to work, this summer, Doc said. I guess that's best.

June 24th.

I wonder if I get to name the baby. I hope so. If it's a girl, I'll name it Juliet. Sort of after me, but more romantic. I don't know about a boy. I'd kind of like to name a boy for my father . . . but Clement? Ugh. Or for Doc Therrian, who's been so great . . . but *Clarence*? Double ugh. Well, I'll just hope it's a girl. Probably I won't get to choose the name anyway.

July 30th.

It's so *hot*. And I'm so *huge*. When my mother looks at me, she cries, sometimes. They've enrolled me in a fancy boarding school for next year. Miss Somebody's.

152

August 1st.
Good news! Doc Therrian says they've found a terrific family who wants to adopt my baby! They won't tell me who, of course. In fact, Doc doesn't know. But it's being set up with a lawyer, and Doc said that the parents are terrific people, according to the lawyer, and that they can't have a baby of their own.

Later
When I wrote that, I thought it *was* good news. Now, the more I think about it, the more I think I don't want anyone else to have my baby. It *is* mine. Maybe there's some way I could keep it. We'd be just fifteen years apart. It would be like having a brother or a sister.

August 8th.
It's weird, being here at the house all summer, with no one knowing. Doc Therrian comes often. He pretends it's a medical visit . . . he always brings his stethoscope . . . but mostly we just sit and talk. We both read a lot, and we talk about books. Or just anything. He tells me about when he was a boy, in Simmons' Mills. Can you imagine living in a place like this, all your life? And we talk about the baby. He says it wouldn't be fair for me to keep it. Not fair to the baby. Funny, I wasn't thinking about the baby, just about myself. He's right, I guess. Those other people are waiting. I wonder if they've bought little clothes.

August 29th.
I feel strange. I keep having pains, and then they turn out to be nothing.

September 10th.

School started in Simmons' Mills. What a strange feeling. All the kids think I am off at boarding school. I can see, sometimes, the Hartley twins riding down the hill on their bikes, heading for the high school in the mornings. If their mother knew how fast they go, she'd kill them. Coming home, they have to get off and walk, pushing their bikes. Hah. I don't think I'd be able to walk up that hill now if you paid me a million dollars.

September 13th.

I've had pains off and on all day. Doc says this is probably it. I'm scared stiff. One thing I made him *promise*. That they'll let me see the baby, and hold it, before they take it away.

September 15th.

It's a girl a girl a girl a girl! I haven't seen her yet, but they told me I will. I was asleep when she was born. Doc Therrian gave me something at the hospital, and the last thing I remember is when they were wheeling me down the hall to the delivery room. Mom leaned over and kissed me. Doc was holding my hand and walking beside the stretcher. When I woke up I was thin again, and achy all over, and Doc was there smiling, and said it was a girl, and she's fine. I'm so tired.

September 17th.

I don't care what Doc says, it isn't fair, it *isn't*. I could keep her. I could get a job, and have an apartment somewhere, and earn enough so that we could live.

Oh, I know, that's stupid, but I just feel so sad. This morning a lawyer came, with the papers. I hated him. Doc was there, and my parents, and we all talked, and before I signed my name, the lawyer said several times, "Now you're sure this is what you want to do?" Why did he keep asking? Of *course* I'm not sure. But in the end I signed where he showed me.

Mom and Daddy signed, too. And then Doc attached another sheet of paper that had *Terry's* signature, all the way from Colorado. Funny. Terry has never written to me. I wonder if he's as miserable as I am about this.

When they had all left, I cried. After a minute Doc Therrian came back in the room, and he put his arms around me and held me. And he cried, too.

September 18th.

Tomorrow I'm going home. So is the baby, wherever her home will be. Oh, I hope they have a little cradle ready for her, and a pink blanket, and lots of bright-colored toys. Tomorrow, Doc says, I can see her, to say goodbye.

September 19th.

I was all dressed, ready to leave, waiting for Mom to come and get me. And the baby was all dressed, too, in clothes that Mom had bought, when they brought her in. They left me alone with her for just a few minutes.

She is so beautiful that when I saw her, I cried.

Then I didn't want her to remember me (do they remember, that little? I don't know) crying, so I smiled at her, and kissed her on the cheek, and said goodbye. I'll never see her again. I guess the thing I hope most for her is that she'll be happy, and never know what it's like to be lonely.

IT WAS what her mother had written, too, to Tallie. "She is so beautiful that when I saw her, I wept."

Do they remember? Julie had asked her diary. No. I don't remember, Natalie thought. If I could, what would

I remember? Being taken from Julie, dressed in the clothes that Julie's mother had bought, taken by whom? Probably Dr. Therrian — delivered to Foster Goodwin's office, and picked up there by Mom and Dad. It wasn't a bad thing. Julie loved me. It was a little-girl, selfish kind of love, the same kind of thing I used to feel for my favorite toys, so that I wouldn't share them with Nancy; or like what I felt for that kitten I had once. I was jealous when it purred and butted against someone else, wanting to be petted; it seemed so important that it be only mine. But Julie *did* love me.

And my parents loved me then, even on that first day when they drove that long road to a strange place to bring me home. Not in the same way Julie did. "She will be her own person," Mom had written about me to Tallie. Mom and Dad have always loved me that way, so that they always let me purr against other people, didn't grab me back and say "She's *ours*." I never realized it until I read what Julie wrote when I was born; she cried — and what she wrote, finally, was "the thing I hope most for her is that she'll be happy" — but Julie was so young. She really wanted to hold on tight to me, saying "*Mine*," the way a child does to a favorite doll, until the doll, sometimes, is broken. She was just old enough that she realized she had to let go, not old enough to know why. And it was the doctor who helped her do it.

Dr. Therrian. I think he loved me, too, when I was born. I wonder why. Dad cares for his patients, many of them in very special ways, but he doesn't love them the way Dr. Therrian seemed to love Julie and her baby.

Because he was lonely, and Julie seemed to be, too?

And now he is more alone than he has ever been, dying. Or dead. I should call Anna Talbot and ask about him.

George, the green-uniformed doorman, recognized Natalie. "Another note?" he asked, smiling at her when she appeared in front of the apartment on 79th Street.

"No," she said. "Mrs. Hutchinson's expecting me."

George opened the door to the building, took her to the brass cage of an elevator, and pressed the button for the sixth floor. When the door unfolded itself at six, Natalie found herself in a small foyer with a parquet floor; large plants sat in thick woven baskets in the corners. The only door was massive and dark, with a polished brass knob. Natalie knocked timidly, and it was Julie who answered.

She was dressed in spotless white slacks and a bulky white cowl-necked jersey; there was a heavy gold bracelet on her right wrist, and her hair was braided in a thick dark coil that was looped into a knot at her neck. For the second time in two days, Natalie had left the hotel feeling chic and lovely and been transformed into tacky awkwardness when she greeted Julie.

"What a lovely suit," Julie said graciously, looking at Natalie's bright red linen. "Come in, come in."

The spacious living room was airy and pale, its walls stark white, the carpet hazy beige, and the few, carefully placed pieces of furniture shades of white, beige, and yellow. On one wall, a lighted painting hung alone; Natalie recognized the ephemeral light and the indistinct brushstrokes of it as an impressionist's. It fitted with the room. So did Julie. Natalie felt like a bright red blotch; she wished she had worn her yellow dress.

"Sit down." Julie smiled, seating herself in front of the small table where tea things were already set out. "The boys will be in, in a moment. I want you to meet them."

They appeared in a doorway, silent and shy, two of them dressed identically in blue cotton shorts and striped jerseys. Dark hair. Dark eyes. They didn't have Julie's eyes, or Natalie's.

"Come in, boys, and be polite!" called Julie. "Natalie, this is Gareth —" the older boy came forward and held out his hand to shake Natalie's — "and this is Cameron. Cam, take your thumb out." The little boy took his thumb from his mouth, and held it, warm and wet, out to Natalie's hand.

"Hey," said Natalie, grinning. "Hi there."

"Who are you?" asked Gareth. Cameron had replaced his thumb.

"I'm Natalie. I'm a friend of your mom's. What are you guys doing this afternoon?"

"Taking our bikes to the park," said Gareth, less shyly. "I have a new bike, with training wheels. Cam just has a tricycle."

"Bet you're pretty fast on your tricycle, aren't you, Cam?" asked Natalie.

Cameron smiled behind his thumb and nodded.

"Here, boys. You may each have a cookie. Then go along with Caroline." Julie held out the plate of fragile cookies; each boy took one carefully, and they left the room. In the doorway, a young woman waited for them. Cameron looked back and waved.

"They're lovely children, Julie," said Natalie, when they had gone.

"Aren't they?" said Julie proudly. "They're bright, too. Gareth's already learning French in school.

"Well," she said, pouring tea into thin white cups. "So you go back this afternoon. Has it been a good trip? Are you glad you came?"

"Yes," said Natalie thoughtfully. "It was important to me, finding you. I suppose if I hadn't, I would have wondered for the rest of my life.

"And I read the diary last night." She took the blue book from her purse and laid it on the table that was between them. "It explained a lot of things."

"It was a terrible year in my life," Julie said. She lit a cigarette and leaned back in the pale yellow chair. "But you know, Natalie — I hope you could tell this from the diary — after the first few months, when it was so hard to believe that I was actually pregnant, well, after that, I never had any bad feelings about the baby. About you, I mean. I really, I think, grew to care very much about what happened to you. For a while there, except for Doc Therrian, you were all that I had. My parents were there, but they never really adjusted to it; they were so sad and ashamed. I was very lonely. But I had the doctor, and I had you, inside me."

"Julie, what happened to Terry? I can't quite bring myself to say 'my father.'"

Julie sighed. "No, I don't blame you. Poor Terry. You

know, I really can't even remember him very well. I think he was a nice boy. Very bright; very handsome. But he was young, too, and he hated Simmons' Mills, as I did, even though he'd lived there all his life. There was that bond between us for the short time we knew each other, that we both felt outside of the town. He became absolutely panicked when I realized I was pregnant. There was so much he wanted to do with his life, and suddenly — well. I can't blame him for any of what happened. I never saw him again. He went to Colorado that summer, and than he decided to stay out there and go to college. The following year, when I was at Miss Sheridan's, my parents heard somehow, I suppose from friends in Simmons' Mills, that Terry had been killed in an accident out west. I felt sad, but not much more, when I heard it. It was as if the whole thing had ended, then. You were gone, and then Terry was gone. I thought about writing to his father, but I never did. I just concentrated on my own life after that: I think my main goal after that year was that I should never, ever again, be lonely or feel out of place."

Julie smiled suddenly. "I succeeded, too. Look — did you notice those?" She gestured with her hand to the far wall of the room.

Natalie stood up and walked across the long room to the white wall that was covered with framed photographs of Julie. Some of them were magazine covers. Others were portraits signed by famous photographers: there was Julie laughing; Julie pensive, with her head tilted down into shadows; Julie regal, with bare shoulders and a diamond necklace; Julie flirtatious, glancing with half-closed eyes over her shoulder; Julie maternal, holding an infant against her as she looked into its sleeping face.

"You're sure," asked Julie, coming to stand beside Natalie, "that you wouldn't want a career like that?"

Natalie looked at the wall for a long time. There must have been thirty separate Julies there: all of them posed, all of them paper.

"Very sure," she said finally. "But you know, Julie, I wish Dr. Therrian could see these. It's too late now, of course. He may not even be alive. But when I talked to him, I could tell how much he cared about you. He must have wondered, all those years, how you were, whether you were happy."

They sat back down. The tea remaining in Natalie's cup was cold.

Julie lit another cigarette. "He never actually told me this," she said suddenly, "but I am quite sure that he wanted very much to keep you himself. I could feel, all that summer, that it was on his mind. I hoped he would suggest it, but at the same time I knew it wouldn't have worked. He was in his sixties, then, and his wife's health was bad."

Natalie thought of the old man, dying, all alone. And if he had adopted her? At least he would have had a daughter there to tell him goodbye. She didn't wish that for herself. But she remembered him there, in the hospital bed, and how he had looked at her with fondness and false recognition, and said, "Julie?" She wished it, in a way, for him.

"It must be awful, having no family," she said. "Mrs.

Talbot told me that their only child had died very young."

Julie stared at her, puzzled. "You mean he didn't tell you?"

"Tell me what? We only talked about you, and about me."

"Oh, Natalie, I didn't realize. I thought you knew. The diary didn't explain, about Doc Therrian?"

"Explain *what*?"

"Terry. His real name was Peter Therrian. He was Doc Therrian's son."

BRANFORD WAS greener, cooler than New York, and quieter; the smells of Branford were newly mown lawns, trimmed hedges, and the fresh wet-and-rubber scent of sprinklers. The city with its combined scents of exhaust fumes and leather taxi seats seemed far behind Natalie.

And Tallie was there: on the porch, in the swing. She beamed when she saw Natalie.

"Darling!" she greeted her. "Can you believe that here I am, ensconced like an old lady, like a *grandmother*, being waited on hand and foot? Your mother convinced me to come. Just for two weeks. Then I'm back to the island in time to see fall come; I wouldn't miss fall on the island for anything! But I'm so glad you're back; I love that red suit with your dark hair. Perhaps I'll do a sketch of you while I'm here."

Kay Armstrong came to the porch and hugged Natalie.

"I just couldn't bear staying away any longer, so I persuaded Tallie to come back with me for a little while, at least. Welcome home, Natalie. You girls did a terrific job while I was gone. I can't find a *thing* in the kitchen, but everything is so tidy and clean."

Nancy appeared at the door, with a tray. "Iced tea, everybody! Hey, Natalie's back! Take my glass, Nat, and I'll get one more."

They sat, sipping from the tall glasses that clinked with the brittle splinters of ice: three generations of women, on the Armstrongs' porch. Tallie was poised and graceful on the swing, her face as strong as sculpture; beside her, Kay sat, relaxed, tanned, and happy, and held her mother's hand un-self-consciously. Natalie and Nancy sprawled on the steps; Natalie kicked off her city shoes and stretched her bare feet beside her sister's.

In the dim woodsy place at the end of the lawn, tree frogs and doves made the settling sounds that came always at twilight in summer.

"I think," said Nancy, "that if I could choose anyplace to be at all, I would choose here. Right now, anyway."

"Me too," said Natalie.

"Me too," agreed their mother.

Tallie was silent. Finally she said, "I don't know. I think I'd choose a place from the past. I'm delighted to be here, of course, but there are all these memories that I yearn sometimes to go back to."

"Memories are always better, though, than the actual time was," said Nancy. "Don't you think so?"

"I think you're right, Nancy," said Kay Armstrong. "Because you can filter out the bad parts. Like if I were to remember this moment, ten years from now, I'd censor the mosquito that's biting my ankle at this very moment. Damn!" She reached down and slapped her foot.

"And I'm censoring, right at this instant, the fact that I have to go to the bathroom." Natalie laughed.

"Where's your sense of romance, you people?" hooted Tallie from the swing. "You should learn to practice mind over matter. That wasn't an insect, Katherine. It was simply an affectionate nibble at your ankle. And Natalie, you simply are filled with a wonderful sense of warmth and fullness. That's how I operate *my* memory. I simply remember everything, and translate it as I wish. You should all learn that process of selectivity."

"I'll be back in a minute," said Natalie. "I'm going to think about that in the bathroom. I have this marvelous sense of warmth and fullness."

From the hallway inside the front door, she could hear Nancy say, "Isn't it good, having Natalie back?"

One more trip, she thought. I have to make only one final trip.

33 NATALIE LEFT her father's office for a moment on Tuesday morning to help an elderly woman patient into her taxi. Mrs. Pittman had been coming to Dr. Armstrong for years; now she was increasingly frail, a combination of age and illness, and her mind had begun to wander more often into the past than it

stayed in the present, as if the memories were a more comfortable place to live.

"Do you have someone to help you into the house when you get home, Mrs. Pittman?" Natalie asked, feeling the woman's hand trembling and fragile in hers.

"Frederick helps me," Mrs. Pittman whispered, as if it were a secret. She clutched at the black coat she wore, despite the August heat.

Natalie knew that Frederick, her husband, had been dead for years. He had run the little drugstore where she had bought ice cream and comics as a child; she remembered when he had been hit and killed by a bus in front of the drugstore on an icy evening. She had cried at the news, remembering the kindly man who always confided in her that Casper the Friendly Ghost was his favorite, too. She had been ten at the time.

"Frederick's not there now, Mrs. Pittman," Natalie said gently. "Isn't it your landlady who helps you?"

The old woman looked puzzled, and plucked imaginary dust from her coat sleeve. "Oh," she said. "Yes. Yes, of course."

She brightened suddenly, and said, "Wouldn't you come to have dinner with me some night, dear? I make such a nice pot roast."

Natalie helped her into the back seat of the taxi, and handed her the big shopping bag filled with sweaters, apples, and newspapers that she always carried. "Maybe sometime." Natalie smiled. "You take care of yourself, now."

Mrs. Pittman had forgotten her. "I could make you

an apple pie," she was saying, but she was saying it to the taxi driver.

They drove away.

Natalie found her father in the small lab, drinking a quick cup of coffee between patients.

"Dad, what's going to happen to Mrs. Pittman? She's all alone. I hate putting her in that taxi and knowing she's going back to an empty apartment."

Dr. Armstrong sighed. "I've just been talking to her niece on the phone," he said. "I guess they're going to put her in a nursing home. It's not the ideal thing, but what else is there? She has no children. The other relatives don't want to have her live with them. I feel fairly certain she's due to have a massive stroke soon. If she were younger, or if her health were better, there would be the possibility of surgery, but — oh, I don't know. It's frustrating, sometimes. They are so many old people like that, with no one. The interesting thing is that they don't fear death as much as they fear being alone. Florence Pittman, for example, fends off the loneliness by pretending her husband is still alive."

"Oh, I wish he were."

"Well, if he were, her physical condition would be the same. But at least she wouldn't be trying to face things all by herself. There's just so much a doctor can do."

He rotated his coffee cup gently in his hand, watching the cream blend slowly into the coffee.

"Natalie, do you remember the time that infant was brought in here, the one that had died during its nap?"

Natalie nodded. "I'll never forget it."

"When I was a student, and then when I was just beginning in practice," her father said slowly, "the death of a child was the one thing I couldn't get used to. It seemed so cruel, so unnecessary, such a waste. For a while I thought I would become a pediatrician, just so that I could do my best to prevent such things."

"But you didn't. Why not?"

He looked at her and chuckled. "To be perfectly honest, I found that I hated dealing with chicken pox and diaper rash.

"But—" He sipped his coffee. "More than that. I began to be aware that when something devastating strikes a young person, a child, it is almost always mitigated by the fact that there is a family. People who care, who comfort, who grieve. That doesn't make illness, or pain — or death — any less cruel or frustrating, but it makes those things bearable. Like that baby. It was a tragic thing for those parents — who, incidentally, Nat, had another baby this past spring — but still, that infant, when he died, was in a warm and happy home. His life, short though it was, was filled with love. Do I sound sentimental?"

"Yes." She smiled. "I like it."

Dr. Armstrong frowned. "But it's the old people, the ones who have no one, who touch me now. I do what I can for them medically, and sometimes it isn't much. But more than that, I listen to them, care about them. I even sent Florence Pittman some flowers on her last birthday. She was eighty-seven." He looked a little sheepish.

"Dad, I love you so much."

"I know that, Natalie. But thank you for saying it."

"Dad. You know that I've spent the whole summer — well, looking for things, figuring things out?"

He nodded.

"You haven't ever asked what I've found."

"Natalie, your mother and I knew that if you wanted to tell us, you would. It's not a decision we can make for you. If you don't ever want to tell us, we'll understand. We'll accept that."

"I'm not sure I want to tell you all of it. But there's this one thing. I found a man, an old man. He was very sick when I saw him last month, and I'm not even sure if he's still alive. He has cancer. And he was just like you were saying, all alone. He had no family left, and he was in a hospital, dying, with a few plants and flowers friends had sent. And the green hospital walls."

Her father looked at his empty cup. "I know," he said. "I mean I know what's it's like. I've seen it again and again."

"But, Dad," said Natalie slowly. "I didn't know it then, but now I've found out that he's my grandfather.

"So I have to go back. Just one more trip, to see him. I'm a little afraid to; I'm afraid that he'll be gone, that I'll go back only to put flowers on a grave. But I have to do at least that."

"Natalie, if you'd like me to, I'll find out for you. If you call the hospital, they'll only give you the official information: his condition is poor, or satisfactory. But if I call, as a doctor, I can find out what's really going on. Do you want to tell me his name and the name of the hospital?"

She wrote it for him. Clarence Therrian, Simmons' Mills Community Hospital, and he looked at the piece of paper and smiled.

"I remember Simmons' Mills," he said. "We drove there, your mother and I, and you were waiting, wrapped in a yellow blanket, sound asleep."

"Dr. Armstrong," said his nurse crisply from the door to the lab, "there are patients waiting in *every* examining room."

Natalie and her father grinned at each other.

"Thank you, Dad," she said.

At the end of the long, busy day, Natalie was tidying up the waiting room before she went home. Dr. Armstrong finished making notes in a patient's folder, closed it, and said, "Natalie, tell your mother that I'll be late for dinner. I have to check on a patient in the hospital before I come home."

"All right," said Natalie.

"And I'm giving you the next two days off, Nat. I made that phone call. Clarence Therrian is still alive. But I think you'd better go tomorrow. Don't wait for the weekend."

She was saddened. She knew he was dying, had even expected that he might be dead. But suddenly she was more saddened by it than she had been before.

"Does he know, Natalie? That you're his grand-daughter?"

"Yes."

He turned to leave, stopped, came back, and put his arms around her for a moment.

"Natalie," he said, sitting down on one of the waiting room chairs, "I have an apology to make to you. At the beginning of the summer, when you set off to make this search, I was disturbed by it. Hurt. So was your mother. You knew that, of course.

"But we were wrong, I think. I can't speak for Mom, but I suspect you'll find she's come to realize the same thing I have. That it was the right thing for you to do."

"Dad," said Natalie, puzzled, "I'm not even sure of that myself."

He was silent. "It's a fine line," he said finally, "and I've been thinking about it a lot — the line between the past and the present. And it's a line we have to feel our way along, so that we know what the connection is. For you, the connections were twisted and blurred. It was the right thing, to sort them out."

"Dad," said Natalie suddenly. "Do you remember the game we used to play at our birthday parties, when we were little? We called it Spiderweb."

He nodded and laughed, remembering. "Sure. Your mother and I spent hours, running threads all around the house, over furniture, behind and under things, and at the end of each thread there was a prize for each child."

"How I loved that. Scrambling around, following that thread. It seemed as if there would be something miraculous at the end of it."

"And was there?"

She laughed. "A pack of gum. Or a comic book. I don't remember the prizes as much as I remember the excitement of looking for them."

"Does this summer seem like a Spiderweb?" her father asked.

"A little, maybe. The challenge of looking. The fear that the thread might break. Expecting the miracle."

"And finding it?"

Natalie shrugged. "Finding the ordinary."

"Very often, you know," her father told her, "after those birthday parties, your mother and I would end up throwing away the packs of gum, the comic books. The kids would forget to take them home. As you said, the prizes weren't as exciting as the searching."

"I *did* find my mother — my natural mother, Dad," Natalie said suddenly. "I won't forget that."

"Of course you won't. How will you fit it into your life, Natalie?"

"I already have, I guess. I said hello to her, and I said goodbye to her. I won't *forget* her. But she's not part of my life anymore."

Dr. Armstrong lit his pipe, and the thin blue streak of smoke lifted itself toward the ceiling of the waiting room. "Natalie, you've done a very healthy thing. People like Florence Pittman don't ever say goodbye to the past. Saying goodbye is the hardest part, and some people never learn how."

"She loved her husband so much, Dad."

"I know. And your mother and I love you. But we'll have to say goodbye to you, in a way, when you go off to college. You have to let go when the time comes. If you don't, you live with ghosts, the way Florence Pittman does."

"And Tallie," said Natalie suddenly, stabbed with a sharp pain of disloyalty.

Her father chewed on the stem of his pipe, and nodded. "And Tallie. She still lives surrounded by memories of Stefan. But Tallie's ghosts are happy ones, Nat. Not the confused and painful ones that make Florence Pittman's life difficult. And not the same kinds as yours."

"It's been a strange summer, Dad. And now there's just Dr. Therrian. There are others, I guess, but he's the one I want to make the connection to, the one I want to say goodbye to."

"Is it because he has no one else?"

"Partly that, I guess," she said. She thought for a moment. "But mostly — I didn't realize this till now, Dad — mostly it's because he loved me so much that he said goodbye, and let me go."

34 NANCY WENT with Natalie to Simmons' Mills. It was Natalie's idea.

"What the heck," said Nancy when her sister suggested it. "Steve's mad at me, as usual. I'm sick of babysitting for the Kimballs every minute. That kid of theirs always wants twelve bedtime stories and fourteen glasses of water, and then when he wets the bed, guess who has to change the sheets. Sure, I'd love to take a couple days off from my life."

The trip seemed shorter with company in the car. Nancy chattered endlessly about everything, about nothing.

"You should have said yes, Nat, when she asked you if you wanted to be a model. Wow. Think of all the money. Think of all the *men*, lusting after your face on the cover of *Vogue*."

Natalie grimaced. "Look there to the left, Nance, at the mountains."

Nancy glanced at the jagged, desolate peaks against the thin haze of the August sky. "Wow," she said.

"It's about your vocabulary." Natalie laughed. "Do you think you could come up with a better expletive than 'Wow' occasionally? Maybe Horrible Aunt Helen will give you a thesaurus for Christmas and you could investigate some other possibilities of language?"

Nancy giggled. They rounded a sharp curve in the road and the mountains disappeared behind a thick barrier of spruce trees.

"Hey, I wasn't kidding, Nat. You could make a fortune, being a model. I'll be back in Branford, being a nursery school teacher or something, probably married to Steve and having kids that wet the bed every night, and I could pick up glamorous magazines and say, 'That's my sister on the cover.' I'd tell my kids, 'Look at Aunt Natalie, there in the centerfold of *Playboy*. Isn't she gorgeous? She's the one who sends you those expensive toys from New York every Christmas.'"

"Not me, Nance. You can say, 'Look there, kids, on the cover of *Time*. That's your brilliant Aunt Natalie with the thick glasses. She's just discovered a cure for Rocky Mountain Spotted Fever and they've awarded her the annual Lady Doctor prize. She's the one who sends you all those yucky vitamin pills at Christmas.'"

Nancy groaned. "You have no sense of adventure, Natalie."

"Come on, that's adventurous, being a doctor."

"You could have Paul Newman on your doorstep. Robert Redford. Elton John."

"Maybe I will anyway. They can come when they have hernias to be repaired."

"Gross. Well, maybe you can write a book and make your fortune that way. *Probing the Innards of the World's Most Gorgeous Men.* That would really sell, Nat. What is Redford's appendix really like? Buy this book for $12.95 and find out."

"*Scars of the Stars*, I'll call it."

"And the *Reader's Digest* will present the condensed version. The minor operations."

"We're almost there, Nancy."

"Almost where, to the *Reader's Digest*? You haven't even written the book yet."

"Almost to Simmons' Mills. Just over the top of this hill. Look."

She slowed the car at the top of the hill, and they looked down. There was the town again, unchanged: the small main street beside the river, the gray buildings huddled in the cleared rectangle carved from the vast forest, the blur of paper mill smoke thick from its tall chimney, discoloring the sky.

"That's where I was born," said Natalie.

"Wow," said Nancy softly. "I mean, *wow*."

|35| NATALIE WENT to the hospital alone, leaving Nancy at Mrs. Talbot's, perched on a kitchen stool with her feet twisted around its rungs, watching Anna Talbot make brownies for the church fair.

"I'll wait here," Nancy had said. "I hate hospitals. And he won't want to see me anyway. Just you."

"Tell him Anna sends best regards," Mrs. Talbot had said, and confided, "I sent him a card last week. Of course, the nurses may not have told him who it came from. They do that sometimes; nurses can be so secretive. You ask him, dear, if he got my card, won't you?"

"Certainly," Natalie had lied, and walked along the quiet, tidy main street of Simmons' Mills to the hospital where Clarence Therrian was dying. She saw the town now through Julie's eyes. She saw the teen-agers, standing on the corner by the drugstore, laughing in a small group, who came to an abrupt silence and averted their eyes as she walked past; they had done that, once, to the pretty young girl from another city who came to Simmons' Mills and couldn't find a way to make friends. Who wore her socks up; or was it down? Today none of them had socks on at all. They wore sneakers, sandals, or were in bare feet. It didn't matter. If Julie had arrived at Simmons' Mills today, she would still have been out of place; they would have lapsed into silence as she walked past, would have looked the other way. And Julie, young, vulnerable, hurt, would not have known to smile, to joke with them, to search for some place of common laughter and circumstances where they could have been friends.

"Hey," said Natalie suddenly to the tall, thin, arrogant-lipped boy balancing himself, rocking back and forth, on a garish motor bike in front of the drugstore. "That's a cool bike."

He looked over at her and grinned shyly. The hostile arrogance fell away from his face. "Yeah," he acknowledged proudly. "I got it for graduation. Man, can it go."

The boys grouped nearby laughed. "Varrroooom," they said in unison, mimicking the sound of the bike. "You should see him. He's a speed freak, man."

"Wanna ride?" the boy asked her. "I won't go too fast."

Natalie laughed. "No thanks," she said. "I have to go someplace. It's a terrific bike, though."

She walked on, and they waved casually to her.

Damn, thought Natalie. Why didn't you *try*, Julie? They didn't really care how you wore your socks, or your hair. If you had just smiled. Joked with them. Tried to find out what kind of people they were.

And if you had? Natalie smiled. Where would *I* be? Nowhere. She walked on.

Doctor Therrian looked, thought Natalie suddenly as she stood beside his bed, like a rag doll left behind in the yard of a summer cottage after the August occupants had gone: discolored by rain, faded by sun, drained by the passage of time and by being forgotten. She felt like the child who had made a long trip back to find something she loved. The ravages didn't matter, because it was still there; that was the important thing.

"Doc," she said softly, calling him by the name Julie had; but he didn't move. The eyes were closed in his gray, wasted face. But he breathed. Quietly; evenly. She sat down beside his bed and took his hand.

"Doc. It's Natalie. Do you remember? I'm Julie's daughter. I'm the one who was born here, to Julie Jeffries, and to Terry."

Quietly his breaths came, and the hand in hers was very still. She rubbed it gently, feeling the bones and veins through the loose gray shroud of skin.

"I came before, Doc, and you thought I was Julie. I look like her. I have blue eyes the way Julie does.

"You helped me find her. She lives in New York, now, and is happy. She has two beautiful little boys.

"And she told me about you. How you helped her, when she was so young and so scared. She could never have gotten through that summer without you, Doc. You must have known that. You used to come to see her. You pretended they were medical visits; but it was just to talk, wasn't it, Doc? You knew how frightened she was."

He didn't move. The lines in his face were like the furrows she had seen in the fields at the beginning of summer; like the deep primordial cracks in the glacial rocks of the mountains she had seen from the road to Simmons' Mills.

"And it was because I was your grandchild, wasn't it, Doc? Julie told me that you cried, too, when the lawyer took me away.

"But I came back to tell you that you did the right thing. Maybe you've wondered about that all these years. But I've had a happy life, Doc. I have a family, the best kind of family, and next month I'm going to college. I'm going to be a doctor, like you, and like my father.

"The only thing I never had was a grandfather. At least

I *thought* I didn't. When Julie told me that you were my grandfather — well, it's why I came back."

She stroked his hand. His quiet breathing didn't change.

"I want to tell you something else, Doc," she said finally. "That I'm sorry about your son. You must have loved him very much, even though he made some mistakes. It must have been so hard, losing him.

"But you have me, still," she said, holding his fragile hand against her cheek. "I'm so glad I found you, Doc, so that I could say goodbye."

She kissed his hand, put it down, and left him there, with whatever he had heard, whatever he remembered, and whatever he was dreaming.

36 KAY ARMSTRONG WAS ironing in front of the television, watching an afternoon quiz program as she attacked a heavy linen tablecloth with the iron.

"Mom, you're incredibly bourgeois sometimes," said Natalie, peeling the fuzzy exterior of a peach carefully with her teeth. "Classy people never watch quiz programs."

"Classy people eat peaches with small polished silver forks. If you're going to stay in this room you have to be quiet. I'm winning everything on this program."

"I want to tell you something," said Natalie, slurping as she bit into the peach.

"Shhhh. I've won a sewing machine and a wig and a year's supply of something, I forget what."

"What did you have to answer to win the sewing machine?"

"The capital of Albania."

"Ha. You don't know that. *Nobody* knows the capital of Albania."

"*I* do. That dreadful lady with the big teeth and bleached hair didn't, and she really *wanted* the sewing machine, too."

"What is it? The capital of Albania?"

Her mother grinned. "*I'll* never tell. You're dripping on your shirt."

Natalie wiped her shirt with her paper napkin. "Can you quit watching that show for a minute? I want to tell you something."

Kay Armstrong sighed and turned the television off. "It had better be important. They were going to give away a sports car on the last question."

"That's all we'd need. You'd be drag racing down at the supermarket parking lot. I wanted to tell you that I found the woman who gave birth to me."

They looked at each other. Natalie wiped the peach juice from her chin and smiled.

"You mean you really found your mother, Natalie?"

Natalie shook her head slowly. "That wasn't what I said. I said I found the woman who gave birth to me. *You're* my mother."

"Tirana."

"What?"

"Tirana," said her mother again. "It's the capital of Albania. You can have the sewing machine I just won."

"Want a bite of my peach?"

They shared what was left of the dripping peach, slurped in unison, and laughed.

37 TALLIE WAS ALL packed and ready to return to Ox Island. Natalie stood on the front porch and looked around her with a grin at her grandmother's things; packing, for Tallie, consisted of flinging scarves, bracelets, sandals, books, and her odd assortments of clothing into several canvas bags. Then she arranged the disorder at the open top of each bag carefully, so that the disarray took on a kind of precise symmetry. Today the Armstrongs' porch was a still life of Tallie's leavetaking.

Everybody's going away, thought Natalie sadly.

Paul's going next week, and he and I will have to figure out some sort of goodbye to say to each other. The kind of goodbye that covers over the fact that we're not as close as we were when school ended, but that leaves open the possibility that we may be again, someday. We'll kid around a lot, not say the things we both want to, promise to write letters that neither of us will write, joke about things from the past that aren't as important as we once thought they were, and give each other a big hug that makes up for everything else.

Becky and Gretchen will go, and when we say goodbye we'll probably cry, all three of us, but the tears won't mean anything more than: Hey; it was fun being friends. Let's stay friends even though our lives are going in different directions now.

Nancy appeared on the porch, barefoot, scratching a mosquito bite on one leg with her opposite foot. Behind her, Tallie came through the screen door with her hands full of last-minute treasures to take back to the island. She surveyed her bags with a critical look, and rearranged a paisley scarf on the top of one so that its silk folds draped artfully against the faded canvas handle of the bag. On top of the scarf Tallie placed a book of Yeats' poetry; then she inspected the effect, wrinkled her nose, removed the book, and arranged a folded blue sweater in its place.

"There," said Tallie with satisfaction, looking at the bag. She tucked the small volume of poetry into the wide pocket of her woven shawl.

Natalie and Nancy watched her affectionately and shook their heads.

"Tallie," said Natalie, "you're amazing. When *I* pack, I fold every single thing neatly and put it in a suitcase as if I were doing a jigsaw puzzle. The underwear in one section, and the shoes someplace else, and the jewelry all carefully in its own special box —"

"Did your mother teach you to do that?" Tallie looked surprised. "Goodness. I never taught *her*. I wonder how these things come about."

"No," said Natalie ruefully. "My mother travels the way you do. Like a gypsy. And *Nancy* —"

Nancy groaned. "Oh, don't even talk about the way I pack. I couldn't possibly do it the way Mom and Tallie do because I'd end up with shoes that didn't match and I'd forget half of what I wanted to take. So I try to be neat, like Nat. But I find myself anyway, two days later, with everything thrown in upside-down. It's a good thing I hardly ever *go* anyplace, because I'd probably wind up stealing hotel towels without meaning to. I'd just roll everything in a ball, toss it in my suitcase, and when I unpacked, I'd discover I was a thief."

"Not a thief," said Natalie. "Just a slob."

"Okay. A slob, then."

"A good-hearted slob, of course."

"Yeah." Nancy grinned. "I wonder what makes us all so different, though."

No one had an answer.

"Oh, Tallie," said Natalie suddenly, "I hate saying goodbye."

"Don't, then," said Tallie placidly. "*I* never do."

(Do you see a green panther? thought Natalie.

What green panther? I don't see anything at all.)

"But you can't just *pretend* about everything, Tallie."

"Of course you can. If you don't like things, shrug them away."

"Oh, Tallie." Natalie sighed, smiling. "Your life has a kind of magic to it."

Dr. Armstrong came through the screen door onto the porch, making notes in the small book he always kept with him. "Who's talking about magic?" he asked. "I'll tell you what's magic: penicillin. The Ferguson boy's going to be all right, Nat. I've just talked to the hospital."

"Dad, that's *terrific*." Alan Ferguson had cut his hand on a barbed wire fence and treated the cut with two Band-Aids and a casual laugh. Three days before, he had been admitted to the hospital with a temperature of 105 degrees and his arm purple and swollen to the shoulder.

Dr. Armstrong closed his notebook and put it in his pocket. "If anyone should happen to call here for me, have them call the answering service. Dr. Phillips is taking any emergencies for me this weekend."

His daughters nodded.

"All set, Tallie?" He looked at the collection of overflowing bags with a grin.

"My goodness, Alden, someone with your intelligence should know better than to ask a question like that. What does it *mean*, after all: 'All set'? All set for life? For the unexpected? For the disastrous? For the various insanities of the world?"

Dr. Armstrong hugged her, laughing, picked up the largest two bags, and carried them to the car. From the porch, Tallie and the girls saw him lift the paisley scarf from its precisely graceful pattern and fold it tidily beneath the blue sweater.

"Well," remarked Tallie good-naturedly, "beauty is such a transient thing, always. That's one of the reasons I must get back to the island right away. Some of my favorite flowers have already gone, and next thing I know some of my favorite birds will be thinking about flying south, and heavens, what is this, the end of August? Any *minute* the leaves will be changing color —"

She was still talking as she got into the car.

"Where's Mom?" asked Nancy suddenly. "You can't go without telling Mom goodbye, Tallie."

"Don't be silly," hooted Tallie. "Kay's upstairs in the middle of a project that I suggested. She knows I'm leaving. I gave her a huge hug before I came down. Hugs are important. Goodbyes are not. Will you girls please promise me that you will listen to the opera every Saturday when the season starts?"

"Okay," said Natalie and Nancy, uncertainly.

"Liars, both of you." Tallie laughed. "What's the matter, Alden, won't the car start?"

Dr. Armstrong chuckled, started the car, and backed out of the driveway. Tallie's hand fluttered in a wave, the sun in bright explosions on her gold rings and bracelet, but her head was turned; she was talking to her son-in-law; she didn't see her granddaughters wave back.

Kay Armstrong appeared in an upstairs window and raised the screen. "Have they gone? Did Dad fit all of Tallie's things into the car all right?" She saw the car moving down the street and waved.

"Mom!" shrieked Natalie. "Your arm is dark blue!"

"Goodness," said her mother, examining the arm. She extended the other as well. "They both are. Well, this is going to sound a little bit crazy, but Tallie had this idea, you see —"

Nancy groaned. Natalie began to laugh.

"— that perhaps if I took those pale pink sheets — you know the ones that I bought on sale and then hated? Because they looked like birthday party tablecloths for a kindergarten? — and dyed them dark blue, they would seem more elegant. Have a little more joie de vivre."

"Did it work?" asked Natalie dubiously.

"Well, I *think* so. I just hung them on the clothesline, and they do seem to have a distinct *flair* to them. But the problem is —"

"That you've dyed your arms blue," said Nancy.

"Well, that too. I hadn't even noticed that. It's the bathtub."

"The *bathtub*?"

"I think I wouldn't mind, really, if I had dyed the bathtub blue. But for some reason the bathtub is *purple*. Do you girls think you would mind having a purple bathtub? Come and look."

"The only thing I mind," whispered Natalie as she went into the house with her sister, "is never knowing what the heck is going to happen next."

"Well," suggested Nancy, "maybe it's more fun that way. Maybe Tallie was right, about how it's impossible to be 'all set.' I mean, there *are* people who seem to be all set for everything, but they seem to be kind of boring, don't you think?"

Natalie thought about it briefly. "Nancy," she said, "you may be smarter than I give you credit for."

She could hear them from her room: her mother and sister, giggling together in the bathroom as they tried to deal with the purple disaster.

"You guys are on your own," Natalie had told them. "That much purple makes my stomach queasy."

Her bedroom was a temporary disaster area as well. An open trunk sat in the center, half-packed for MacKenzie College. Beside it was a large plastic trash can she had brought in from the garage; there were more things in the trash can than in the trunk. On her bed, in uneven stacks, were the things about which she still had to make decisions. Resolutely, Natalie picked up a folded pair of favorite jeans, soft from countless washings and faded to palest blue; she placed them in the trunk. Then she noticed the frayed hole in the seat of the jeans, decided it wouldn't survive another patching, and took the jeans from the trunk and tossed them into the trash can.

She picked up a pizza-stained sweatshirt, threw it into the trash, remembered with a quick surge of nostalgia the day of the great pizza-eating contest when she, Becky, and Gretchen had consumed so much that they felt too fat, finally, even to laugh. She picked up the sweatshirt again and put it into the trunk.

She held Paul's graduation picture in her hands for a long time. The photographer had caught the kind of smile he had given her so often; she smiled back at it fondly, and laid the photograph on top of the clothes in her trunk.

Then Natalie picked up the cover of the ten-year-old *Vogue* magazine that she had torn off as quietly as possible in a back room of the Branford Public Library. Julie's smile, too, was the same smile she had given Natalie: stunningly beautiful, artfully posed, and achingly transient. Natalie pictured her saying breezily, "Darling, I'm going to have to dash" to the photographer after he had taken the picture, the way she had said the same thing to Natalie once, and left her sitting there alone, bewildered, remembering the smile.

She sighed.

She sat, holding the magazine cover, in the wicker chair that had been part of her room all her life, and rocked. From the bathroom she could overhear Nancy and their mother in a noisy, exuberant argument.

"Try Comet," Nancy was saying. "Try Comet."

Her mother groaned. "It won't work. Do you think

things with astronomical names have some kind of super-natural power? Maybe we should try Moon Drops Facial Cream. Or how about Sunkist orange juice?"

They were both laughing. "Mom," said Nancy again, "try Comet."

Natalie could hear them open the cupboard in the bathroom where the can of cleanser was kept. They were quiet for a moment. Then: "It works!" said Nancy. "Look, Mom! It's working!"

"My goodness; so it is." Her mother's voice sounded curiously disappointed. "Well, then. Au revoir, purple bathtub."

So, thought Natalie, touching her toe against the bed so that the wicker chair rocked gently, that's what it all boils down to.

You have to sort everything out.

You have to figure out what you want to hold onto.

You have to acknowledge what is and what was.

And sometimes what never was, at all.

(Goodbye, Green Panther.)

And you have to relinquish things.

Here I am, making lists again. I never wanted to be a list-maker.

She crumpled Julie's picture between her hands, tossed it into the trash can, and got up to attack the piles of clothes and high school treasures on her bed. This stays; this goes to college; this can be thrown away.

It was the throwing away that was the hardest. But she did it, until the trunk was packed, the trash can was filled, and the room was bare of everything except the memories; those would always be there, Natalie knew.